CW01113103

CELEBRITY ISLAND

LASCO ATKINS

authorHOUSE®

AuthorHouse™ UK
1663 Liberty Drive
Bloomington, IN 47403 USA
www.authorhouse.co.uk
Phone: 0800.197.4150

© 2016 Lasco Atkins. All rights reserved.

No part of this book may be reproduced, stored in a retrieval system, or transmitted by any means without the written permission of the author.

Published by AuthorHouse 09/28/2016

ISBN: 978-1-5246-6409-1 (sc)
ISBN: 978-1-5246-6410-7 (hc)
ISBN: 978-1-5246-6408-4 (e)

Print information available on the last page.

Any people depicted in stock imagery provided by Thinkstock are models, and such images are being used for illustrative purposes only.
Certain stock imagery © Thinkstock.

This book is printed on acid-free paper.

Because of the dynamic nature of the Internet, any web addresses or links contained in this book may have changed since publication and may no longer be valid. The views expressed in this work are solely those of the author and do not necessarily reflect the views of the publisher, and the publisher hereby disclaims any responsibility for them.

Please note this is a work of fiction not to offend any family members or friends and/or associates of the celebrities in question. It is all done out of the respect and love I have for them.

"Dedicated to my parents who have both supported me in their own individual ways"

CONTENTS

INTRO ix

1. FILM SET 1
2. WRAP PARTY 5
3. PREMIERE 7
4. MIB 10
5. CEU 14
6. JOURNEY 20
7. ARRIVAL 23
8. DAY 1 26
9. IT BEGINS 32
10. LEGENDS 35
11. CLONE PARTY 41
12. REVOLT 47
13. THE PLAN 60
14. ESCAPE 63
15. RETURN 70
16. REBELS 72
17. VIRAL 78
18. DOOMED 83

27 CLUB 88
OTHER CELEB DEATHS 89
CV CELEBS LIST 90

INTRO

This work is my homage to films and the possibilities of a good story that can be great. I say "just in case" a lot and always thought it would make for a great character name. I also had this idea knocking around my head for the best part of a decade now. And in recent years have had more motivation to write my scripts/books. My four books are all connected in my memories of a time at film school, where I was dreaming big and always made larger budget films on a small budget. Some of the opening scenes are reminiscent of my experiences as an extra/background artiste on epic blockbusters.

I always felt *Lost* should have been set in the Bermuda triangle and felt a huge let down (I wasn't the only one) as the show ended the way it did. The twist was mushed together from a mix of movie twist endings (mainly *Sixth Sense*). I didn't want the same to happen here. I have included two endings since one leaves it open for a sequel and the other a more dark (sad) ending.

This is still one my favourite concepts which could utilize the CG technology of a German CG artist I read about once. She would be ideal to bring the dead celebs back to life. I have even envisioned how the audio could be created.

I hope you dive into this tale as I did when writing it. Like all my stories I know the beginning and ending, but finding the middle and keeping it going is the challenging part. I can even see the film in my head before I write it, but it evolves as I get words to page. The dialogue itself flows from scene to scene as if I'm *spirit writing* at times. The words spilling onto the screen I fall into the scenery and let it take me over. I love these characters, I hope you do too.

CHAPTER 1
FILM SET

HOLLYWOOD 2016

A motorbike is being chased by a train full of bad guys shooting guns at the film's star: JUSTIN CASE. He speeds around a corner revealing a canyon in the background, he launches off a ramp and with his spare hand and shoots at the bad guys. The action is over the top, but no one is hurt even when JC lands awkwardly on his bike. A gasp comes from the entire crew, then cheers as JC pulls away from the stunt. He slides into position hitting his mark, and skidding right up to the camera ending on a close up of him smirking.

The crew burst into applause once the director yells 'Cut!!! Great print it! I'm pretty sure we got it.' They eagerly await playback in video village, as the rest of the crew start to crowd around the monitors. This being the final stunt and last shot of the entire main unit shoot; excitement is in the air to hear those last fateful words. The director turning towards his first assistant director, call it.'

The first AD on the megaphone, 'that is a picture wrap on the yet untitled Justin Case film everyone. Thanks for all your hard work team and see you at the wrap party.'

The whole crew erupt in a cheer and start hugging each other as they have just completed half a year of filming on this big budget action block buster.

It is an emotional day for all, even JC is crying as he pulls up on his motorbike, covered in dust and fake blood. The 1ST AD passes him the megaphone, JC takes it slowly still catching his breath. He wipes sweat, tears and fake blood from his face. 'Wow. (pause) That was probably the biggest stunt of my life. (The crew laugh) I just wanted to thank all the departments, not just the heads, but in particular my stunt team, my director and especially all the assistants who bust their chops when we HOD's (heads of department) take all the credit!'

Everyone cheers again, most clap as if giving a standing ovation. JC looks around at all the crew with a big smile on his face, he gets off the bike, which is ridden away by an assistant. JC takes off his sweaty shirt, revealing six-pack abs underneath and starts hugging all the females of the crew first. They coo as he embraces them one by one.

Susie, one of the make-up girls comes up to him first asks for his autograph and then tries a bit of flirting. 'God Justin I just wanted to say you're such an inspiration for a lot of us cause you respect everyone, even the extras. You're genuinely a nice guy, so maybe we could have a private chat later at the wrap party?'

Justin coolly replies 'sure babe, no probs. You know how I roll, respect all hard workers not just the minions right?' JC is getting distracted by other girls from the crew trying to get his attention. Susie gives him a hug and a peck on the cheek.

JC turns to the other crew and starts shaking hands with the 1ST and the director, they end up hugging him tight. The director takes him aside with his arm around his JC's neck. 'You know Justin; I've worked in this business for a long while now and I think this could be my biggest hit to date. And you know why?'

JC shrugs, but indulges his director one last time on the shoot.

He continues his flattery 'It's you Justin. I mean you're probably the first actor to do the stunts you do and on top of it all, you're a looker. The ladies love you, and us guys we respect you.'

'Thanks boss. Heh, I'm just a humble guy trying to make it in the world. I didn't plan for my life, but it just sorta happened.'

'Well I still can't believe you pulled that last one off, any other actor would've shit his boots by now, but you kid… You're a success story if there ever was one.'

They walk off together and they see JC's agent Tom Wilkins approaching with one of his hands on a mobile handset. The director goes back to his trailer as JC veers off to chat with his manager. He has a big smile on his face and his laughing at the same time. A make-up assistant hands JC a wash cloth for his face, JC takes it and winks at the girl.

'Justin! My buddy old pal! How's it hanging? Guess what? I just had the studio on the line, they been watching the rushes and they keep telling me your gold.'

'Really Tom?'

'They wanna talk 3 picture deal and they wanna have the damn title of this one locked in by tonight at the wrap party. Remember you're not just a movie star anymore. You're one of us. You're in the big league now.'

'Keep sweet talking.' Justin is enjoying getting his ass kissed by his agent.

Tom holds his arms in the air 'how does producer Justin Case sound, huh?'

'I'm liking it, like sweet music to my ears.'

'Here's the thing, we know you're a hit with the ladies and all, but how about in your spare time you come and produce some films opposed to just getting laid all the time.'

'You jealous Tom?'

'Of course I'm jealous; the ladies love you, not me. They just love my money.'

They walk past some more female crew, who stop talking and are just staring at JC. They give little waves.

Tom noticing this, 'see what I mean?'

They are approaching JC's trailer now and JC steps inside keeping his agent outside.

'Don't quit your day job. See ya at the wrap party.' JC shuts the trailer door in his agent's face.

CHAPTER 2

WRAP PARTY

JC pulls up in his Maserati alone with stills photographers going crazy taking hundreds of snaps. JC wears sunglasses so he's not too bothered by the flashing light bulbs. He suavely walks up the stairs to the wrap party of his latest film. A valet has taken his keys and parks up the super-car. Some reporters try to get his attention, but JC is not answering questions at a wrap party, he saves that for premieres. He has his last film completed screening in two weeks' time. He turns around to give the paparazzi something to print, he gives them a salute in honour of his old army days. Just as he turns to go inside he notices some black government SUV's parked behind the crowd. He spots some people sitting inside but can't make them out due to the tinted windows. He shrugs it off and enters the building.

Inside the club JC goes through the room shaking hands and winking at girls, he gets a drink of champagne off a plate from a waiter and sees Tom in a corner with some of the studio heads. As soon as his agent spots him he comes rushing over and grabs JC by the arm leading him to the table. The studio heads have all got very expensive suits and watches on, even some gold rings.

Tom makes the formal re-introduction 'well here he is, the man of the hour, Mr Justin Case.'

The studio heads don't stand up but offer their hands up, some still chomping on Cuban cigars. They grin as they meet this new celebrity of celebrities, thinking about all the dollar bills in their heads.

'Pleasure to see you again gentlemen.'

'As I was telling you earlier, they wanna sign you to multi picture deal starting with this pet project of yours.'

Justin's confused, 'pet project?'

'They mean the untitled Justin Case film.'

'I know what they mean, but this film has been a labour of love of mine for the past 3 years. At first I couldn't get the funding so I started it with my own funds. That's when you guys came in: Distribution.'

'What they are trying to say is they wanna buy the rights off you and nail the damn title tonight!' Tom says this with a big grin.

One of the heads cuts in 'Justin don't take this the wrong way we just gotta make sure this latest investment of ours has got a snazzy title, you hear?'

'I know, the title has been tough to finalize, but I wasn't thinking of a franchise when I started this, it's one role at a time with me.'

He continues 'that's great kid, but the sooner we know how to sell this thing the beta. That's why we need a –'

'Title,' Justin stating the obvious.

'Yeah, that's right. We need one ASAP. Let's brainstorm a little shall we. First let's get some drinks in.' The studio head waves over a waitress and orders the most expensive champagne and whiskeys they have.

The waitress goes behind the bar chats to her manager, who opens up a locked cabinet bringing out Dom Perignon and some 30 year old whiskey.

Back to the meeting, and Justin is coughing slightly due to the heavy cigar smoke at the table. Polite as ever he indulges the fat cats with the ate of his career in their hands. At one point distracted JC looks around the room and spots a MIB (man in black suit, tie & sunglasses) type character standing in the shadows watching JC even when he had to go to the toilet. He doesn't make anything of it now.

CHAPTER 3

PREMIERE

Cut to two weeks later....TCL (ex - Mann's Chinese Theatre).
JC pulls up in a limo with two models on either arm. This time he does have to give the reporters some air time, it's in his new contract. Not that he minds that is. He stops by a few (mainly female) and gives an intelligent yet slightly spiritual answer to everything. As always everyone is smitten by him and he is so charming and sweet with all who come across his path. The models feel the cramps in their jaw after smiling non-stop for minutes at a time.

An Asian American reporter named Lynn Chan is next up. 'I am standing here live on the red carpet for Justin Case's latest release known as the *Cyber Monk*. With his background serving in the army and martial arts training he was a perfect candidate for this role. And here he is now, um Mr Case what is your latest film about what can we expect tonight at the world premiere?'

'Well Lynn (she smiles), firstly call me Justin. Secondly, it's all about a spiritual army vet who becomes a monk since he feels guilty about all the people he's killed in the line of duty. He retreats from the western world to hide out in a Buddhist temple, but is brought back into service since terrorists have hacked the web and try to bring down the government system.'

'Wow, sounds ambitious. Now, you've just completed your latest film which you actually produced from mostly your own money. Why now? Is this the new Justin Case we will be seeing more of?'

The models on his arms are looking bored, one even hides a yawn. JC is enthusiastic as ever regarding talking about his movies and career. 'That's correct Lynn. We just wrapped on my latest pic and should be out early next year, post has already started and it does, as you say, herald a new step in my career. I have signed a 3 picture deal with the studio to write, direct, and star doing my own stunts again.'

She's smitten, 'that's amazing. You are truly a one of a kind. Your claim to fame reminds me a lot of when Jackie Chan became big in Hong Kong then around the world. Are you aware that you have a huge following in Asia as well?'

'No I wasn't Lynn. Well tell them for me I'll have more coming soon.' JC gives her a gunshot with his fingers then veers off to move up the red carpet, the models are at least happy that one interview is done with.

Ms Chan faces her cameraman to give her outro report, 'well there you have it, a humble new rising action star who his not only good looking but has a charming personality to boot. I'm Lynn Chan reporting live from the TCL in Hollywood.'

Flashes of cameras continue blinding every one along the red carpet as JC continues his press leading him eventually inside. His model friends are bored all the way to the door.

Once inside JC roams the room with virtually everyone giving a high five or congratulating him. They head for the bar and order some cocktails. The models leave to go the ladies room. As he is at the bar some groupies come up to him and ask for his autograph. One asks him to sign on her cleavage, he signs happily. As they chat to him he sees a MIB type for the second time, he spots him standing towards the back wall, trying to be unseen. Twice in two weeks this can't be coincidence, paranoid JC walks over to him. The MIB agent talks into his wrist as he spots JC approaching him. A crowd of people appear in front of JC blocking his view.

The fans are relentless; they must have paid a pretty penny to get in here 'Mr Case, we're your biggest fans, we worked with you on Cyber Monk, you do remember us right?'

JC distracted still trying to focus on the mysterious MIB character 'um, yeah sure. Excuse me I'm a bit busy right now can we talk later?' JC gently shoves past them, but as he gets to where the MIB man was standing he's gone. JC looks around the room but can't see him anymore. Surely he was security or something right? Why did he disappear? Who was that guy? As he scans the room he sees his dates at the bar waving at him from across the room. They hold up the cocktail drinks. JC disappointed walks back towards the two beautiful girls and back to his party.

CHAPTER 4

MIB

JC is walking around his brand new luxurious mansion chatting on the phone to his agent regarding details of his next film(s). He peeks outside the windows every once in a while, walking past his glass case (shrine) of his army days. Purple Hearts and silver medals glint in the LA sun.

After the conversation he puts the phone down and hears a car honking outside his front gate. He assumes it might be someone he knows, but it is just some driver honking at two large black SUV's (from the wrap party) since they are blocking part of the road. JC recognizes the type of car and tries to see inside the tinted windows assuming it's the same people that have been at his last wrap party and premiere. He gets on the phone to try a theory of his.

'911. What's your emergency?'

'Police please.'

'Hang on we'll patch your through. Hold the line please.'

'Sure.'

A few seconds pass and a female police woman answers the line. 'Los Angeles police department, how can I help you today?'

'Hi, this is Justin Case in Beverly Hills.'

'Hello Mr Case, we all love your movies here at the station. You're a great entertainer.'

Justin has heard a lot of this recently, 'uh thanks. Listen, I'm calling because these guys have been stalking me for the past two weeks.'

'Define stalking sir?'

'Well they were at one of my wrap parties, then again at a premiere.'

'Uh huh.'

'Well now their parked outside my security gates and they're blocking traffic.'

'We'll send out a unit right away. Anything else I can help you with today?'

'Nah, that's it. Ciao babe.'

'Well if there's anyth-'

JC hangs up the phone as she still chats on the other end. A half hour later the police have two patrol cars pull up next to the black SUV's and approach with their hands on their guns.

A cop shouts the usual routine, 'you in the vehicle step out slowly with your hands in the air.' Nothing happens. 'I repeat anyone in the black SUV step out of the car now!'

One of the windows rolls down and a badge is held out of the vehicle. The cops take a closer look at the badge and become very polite all of a sudden taking their hands off their guns and tip their hats. The black tinted window rolls back up, the patrol cars reverse, turn around and pull away.

JC sees all this and was right all along, they are government agents. Which branch? He doesn't know. What the hell do they want with him? No idea. He does know that they are more important than cops, maybe FBI or DEA? He thinks about calling 911 back but decides against it, instead he goes downstairs and outside to the front of the house. He approaches his security gate with a coffee in his hand; his morning paper is on his driveway already. He picks it up and goes right up to the gate. He stares into the black windows of the SUV's, nothing happens at first. Then one of the doors opens and the MIB agent that was at the two parties approaches Justin. JC takes one step back in case he gets grabbed through the gate.

'Can I help you or something? Why are you following me around? I'm only an action star, I have no political involvement. Plus I'm retired from the army.'

'Mr Case we have been watching you for some time now.'

'What the hell for!' He feels cornered despite having a metal gate in between them.

'Remain calm Mr Case. I am here working for a very powerful organization that would like to have a simple chat with you.'

'A chat! About what?'

'I can say no more, take my card and we can arrange an appointment at your convenience.'

'Appointment? Is this regarding my movies or my army background?'

'In a way - both. I can't say any more. Please call this number and we will explain.' The MIB agent passes a card through the gate.

JC reluctantly takes it, still cautious of this strange *arrangement*. The card is blank on one side so he turns it over; on the back it says CEU (Celebrity Extraction Unit) and a 555 number. He hasn't heard of that department before and he spent 10 years serving as a marine and special (black) ops. As he looks up the MIB agent is already back in his SUV and the two vehicles are pulling off fast. Tire's screeching leaves a black smoke trail and the smell of burning rubber in the air. JC snorts and heads back to his house.

Time passes and JC hasn't seen the MIB or their vehicles anywhere near him since the *exchange* at his mansion gate. He becomes restless and is tossing and turning at night. He looks at the card from time to time. One day he decides to call the number. After the dial tone someone picks up the phone but there is no answer, then all of a sudden a male voice speaks.

'Good day Mr Case. Are you ready to book a meeting with our agency?'

'Well I still don't know what agency you're talking about. I served ten years and never heard of the CEU!'

'I can't tell you who we are or what we do, you will have to come in for that.'

'OK. (pause) When? Where?'

'How about tomorrow?' The voice asks.

JC shrugs, 'I guess.'

'FYI once you meet with us there is no turning back.'

'I still don't have a clue who the hell this is and what you do!'

'It will all be explained to you tomorrow. I will text you the address.'

'You have my mobile number?'

'We have all your information Mr Case. Trust me; you will wanna hear what we have to say.'

'Am I in trouble or something?'

'Oh no nothing like that. See you tomorrow.' The line goes dead and JC hangs up slowly. He looks outside again, but still no MIB.

CHAPTER 5

CEU

JC pulls up to the CEU security barricade and unsure about this situation he talks nervously. 'Uh hi, I'm here for a –'

One of the security guards comes over and scans his face for ID; he doesn't say anything at first, as if a robot. 'You're cleared Mr Case. Park up and enter the main building.' Both guards stand at attention and salute.

'Up there, right. OK.' He pulls off and finds a parking spot directly in front of the building. He gets out of his car and looks around; the neighbourhood looks and sounds peaceful. What the hell is this place? He enters the building cautiously. Automatic sliding doors, naturally. Motion sensors and a metal detector later.

A receptionist sits at a single desk in a spacious clean reception area. She is typing on a high touchscreen and has a blue-tooth like earpiece. Her hair is tied in a top knot, not a bad looker JC thinks to himself. She looks up from her work station, and stands up straightening her suit. The receptionist walks around the desk/table and offers a handshake to JC. Justin obliges before he even speaks. The receptionist has an I-Pad style portable touch screen with her.

'We're all very pleased you decided to come in Mr Case. We apologize if our agents were very direct with you. But you see this is a top secret branch of the NSA, not the NSA itself. It's only because of your military record you're given this privilege.'

'The NSA or the CEU?'

'Indeed Mr Case. The heads are waiting for you inside already.' She ignores his comment not wanting to reveal too much.

'Okey dokey' he remarks sarcastically.

As they walk along the corridor, the conversation concludes. The receptionist holds her I-Pad device out, 'before you enter you must sign this waiver. You must not disclose any information relevant to today or you will be severely punished by the law and possibly even death. Is that understood?'

JC nonchalantly, 'I guess.' He's had worse threats in wartime.

The receptionist grows impatient 'a simple handprint will suffice.'

JC puts his palm on the screen, a bleep is heard. He is finally led through some hallways and past some offices with no visibility inside and then finally to the conference room. Wall monitors (not TV's) cover all sides of the room, showing the stock market and news reports regarding weather in the Bahamas/Bermuda region. Several government officials in expensive suits are sitting around a massive marble table each with touchscreen technology in front of them. The men consist of a leader of the group, a PR/spokes-person and a few others that remain silent throughout. An assistant is sitting in a corner with an I-Pad taking notes. The receptionist directs JC to the end of the table, so he is at the other end all by himself. Again, he is still totally confused.

'Excuse me Mr Case let me introduce to you the leaders of the CEU.'

'Thanks I guess???'

The receptionist exits and the swivel doors shut behind her automatically. JC turns towards the strangers looking at him, without any smiles like it is usually with JC in the room. There is a silence for a few moments where JC can still hear the receptionist walking down the corridor back to her station. JC gulps and tries to make conversation. 'So you guys are-'

'The CEU. You figured out who we are yet?'

'Well I still don't know what the C stands for.'

'Celebrity.'

Justin laughs out loud thinking this is all an elaborate joke, 'well I definitely haven't heard of that before in all my time in the service and if you've seen my record-'

The leader continues with his short answers, 'we have.'

'I guess you're gonna give me some answers sometime soon I hope.'

'We have all the answers, and we have always been around even before the NSA was green-lit so to speak.' He chuckles trying some film lingo.

'Well who the hell are you guys?'

The spokes-man speaks up now, 'easy tiger. We want to offer you the deal of a lifetime.'

'Deal huh? That's what all this about?'

'We can offer to change your life forever; you would be set for all eternity. So to speak.'

Justin leans back confidently, 'what if I don't wanna change my life?'

The leader cuts in again, 'that's what our organization is all about. We are here to make sure you are known in film history for all time.'

'Last time I checked I'm already heading there.'

'This is a different type of opportunity.'

'I'm listening,' intrigued JC decides to pay attention and be less cocky for once.

The leader goes through the procedure, 'once you agree to this arrangement of ours your life will never be the same.'

JC stands up annoyed for all the vagueness. 'Are we gonna quit beating around the bush or what?'

'Calm yourself Mr Case; this is a unique possibility to change your life and to be a hero to the nation.'

'Hero eh? I like the sound of that,' his ears perk up. JC sits down very slowly.

The CEU leader pushes a button and the lights dim down, one of the walls becomes a massive projection screen playing a promotional video for some island in the Bermuda triangle. It shows scientists doing some kind of genetic engineering and cloning humans. The video plays for a minute then pauses, the lights come back up and JC is baffled.

'Heh, this is nice and all, but what's it got to do with me?'

'We have chosen you Mr Case.'

'Chosen?'

'Not many celebrities have this offer from us. Due to your military background we considered you to be an elite candidate. An exception.'

'Candidate for what? Genetic cloning? Manipulation?'

'What we do at our facilities is way more advanced than anything the human race is aware of, this is not just cloning. It is possibly a new way of life, for the future of mankind.'

'Get to the catch already. What I gotta do so you guys get off my back?'

'It is not that simple. If you sign with us we will give you all the answers for all the questions you have ever asked. But -'

'But what?'

The leader breathes out, 'you would have to leave your life as you know it behind.'

'I'm in pre-production right now for my next film we start shooting in three weeks!'

'We are not saying right now Mr Case we decide when the time is right. What you fail to realize is that we have been behind many celebrity extractions for many years. You would be an exception, a perfect living specimen.'

'OK, let me get this straight. You wanna clone me: Justin Case.'

'Yes precisely.'

'But I gotta leave Hollywood for good?'

The room of CEU men nod their heads in agreement. They think he has taken the bait.

'You guys are all frickin crazy, you know that?!'

'Watch the rest of video then you can make your decision.'

The lights dim again and the video continues, JC is astonished when he sees images of Princess Diana, Bruce Lee, Elvis, Michael

Jackson, members of *27 Club* and many more. There are all walking around on this crazy faraway paradise island. A scientist talks through some of the facilities on the island and the fact that it is completely sealed off from the world and any government affiliations.

JC is impressed by the production quality of the video, it is definitely professionally produced. The camera isn't handheld, but seems to glide somehow. JC can't figure out if it's a dolly or steady-cam. However, he does not believe his eyes regarding the celebrities. Yet when the video ends and the lights come back up JC's jaw is hanging open. He notices it and sits up straight pretending he isn't that impressed.

'So what is your opinion now Mr Case?'

'Cute little video. So next you're gonna tell me that place is for real and you guys fund it, right?'

'We do not discuss where the funds come from but yes it is our division.'

'What if I say no?'

'It is too late for that. By you coming here on your own accord we assume you are the adventurous risk-taking type.'

'You could say that. There's still gotta be something you're not telling me.'

'Well consider this our first and only meeting with you. We won't contact you again regarding this matter. However, this contract is sealed since you will now be entered into the walk of fame. We have already arranged for your star on Hollywood Boulevard, we can have the ceremony in the next month once you fully agree to our terms and conditions. And forever will be one of the island's clones and live in history among all the stars who have died young.'

'Wow, slow down; hold your horses a minute. No one said anything about dying.'

'We mean figuratively of course. Your death is but a metaphor for being a star. Imagine it; you will appear next to James Dean, Kurt Cobain even the late Paul Walker. You can be one of these men if you do as we say.'

'Do I have time to think about this, I mean you guys are saying I have to give up my mansion? My car? My career? What about all the ladies? I can't live without sex.'

'Imagine sleeping with any celebrity you wish: dead or alive. We can make it possible lad.' Hook, line and sinker.

'You mean like clones? Of dead people?'

'Dead if you like, we can attain any DNA we wish. We already have yours by the way.'

'What! How?'

The leader brings up on the info on the table and wall screen. 'You were arrested two years ago for excessive alcohol and drug intoxication. You were swabbed at the station.'

JC has flashback of that night in an LA police station. He always wondered how that story was never leaked to the press. Maybe he was drunk that night? 'Shit. You guys knew about that?'

'Knew about it? We covered it up son. So you see you owe us.'

JC slumps back into his chair, and rubs his hands in his face and through his hair.

'We have the power to destroy your life as you know it or we can give it more life, pardon the pun.'

'K, I get it, I worked for the government before I know what you guys are capable of.'

'So we have a deal then?'

'Do I have a choice?' No other options running through his head.

'Not really. We just wanted to prepare you since your excellent service records have proved you always followed orders without question. This would be your final assignment. Once you work for the US government there is no escape. Once a soldier always a soldier.'

'Yeah I got that vibe.' The table in front of him flashes and blinks a large hand scanner appears in the table. Getting the gist from the receptionist's I-pad JC reaches over to place his hand on the table in front of him. He looks up at the men around the table one last time, then commits.

CHAPTER 6

JOURNEY

TV NEWS REPORT (INCLUDING FOOTAGE OF A CRASH SCENE)

'This is Lynn Chan reporting live from the Hollywood Hills. A day of sorrow as famous actor celebrity Justin Case has died in a car crash late last night. Apparently eye witnesses saw the Maserati in question speed around a corner and launch off of the road. His car exploded and caught fire instantly, his body was burnt beyond recognition. The police authorities have confirmed it was in fact JC's car. We regret he never got to complete his latest franchise which would have surely made him truly a star for all time. RIP Justin, peace be with you wherever you are. That's it for today's top story.'

JC is on a private Naval Base in Florida waiting for his secret plane/helicopter vehicle. He is on the tarmac and it is a nice sunny day. He looks up and hears a faint whirring sound but can't place where the flying vehicle is. A naval employee let's him know his departure vehicle has arrived. JC can't see it anywhere. Then all of a sudden, a cloak is disengaged in front of his eyes, he can't believe it. How tech (nology) has changed in 10 years. JC picks up his army duffle bag and heads towards what looks like a mix between a Huey chopper and a fighter jet (reference: *Avatar & Call of Duty: Advanced Warfare*). He takes one last look around him and waves bye to the only people on the *runway*. Some stand at attention, some salute. The naval employee is guiding the invisible aircraft to prepare for lift off.

JC is guided to his seat by the co-pilot and is strapped in. He peers into the cockpit, where the pilot is engaging the cloak system and preps for launch. Usually this would take a minute for clearances but it is literally seconds. How efficient, JC thinks to himself. In a way he did miss his army days but this was different, this is after he spent years in Hollywood getting big. Somehow this felt like duty, like another spec-ops (special operations) mission. Except this time, he's not supposed to return home. They take off and there is virtually no turbulence during take-off. He hears the engines revving up and can only see flashes of clouds through the cockpit. At first the pressure pulls his head back then it eases up. He feels comfortable in this high-tech plane/chopper unlike his old days flying in *old school* helicopters. At ease he falls asleep, maybe since the low hum of the plane was soothing compared to his memories of army days. A couple hours have passed and next thing he knows he is woken up by alarms and heavy turbulence. Little does he know yet they have to travel through a time warp to get to the island itself. It is similar to a portal and is active only at certain times. That's why they had to leave exactly at the time they did. JC grips the arms on his seat tightly. The co-pilot calls back to JC.

'You OK back there Mr Case?'

JC is feeling a little queasy from the turbulence, it's been a while and this was no ordinary turbulence. He remains silent.

Then the pilot starts talking. 'Don't worry! We'll be outta this time portal in a sec. Don't panic, we do this all the time. It's pretty standard procedure. Except every once in a while-'

'Once in a while what?'

'We get kicked out at the wrong time, no biggie.'

JC gripping onto a handle above him, 'sure! Whatever! Just get us there in one piece huh!'

'On the descent now! Hold on!' They have stopped accelerating and are now dropping down like a roller-coaster ride. JC pukes up in his mouth a bit but swallows it real quick not to let anyone notice. The co-pilot looks back one last time to make sure JC is still alright. He smiles despite the taste of vomit still in his mouth. Ten years since his last drop.

They land with a thud and the co-pilot gets out of his seat and unstraps JC, he then opens up the door and bright white light spills into the cabin. The sound of waves and wind can be heard in the distance. JC takes a moment to re-adjust since he is temporarily blinded by the sunlight. The co-pilot has his helmet and UV visor on so he's fine. JC struggles to find his sunglasses for a second then puts them on. As he steps out of the *unreal ride* the co-pilot calls out.

'Love to stay and chat Mr Case But we got a short window to get back. We got the time portal still open. Nice meeting ya!'

'Thanks for the ride pal.'

CHAPTER 7

ARRIVAL

It is the beginning of *magic hour* as JC steps out onto the landing platform (Helipad) on the east coast of the Island. The co-pilot shuts the door and literally within seconds the vehicle takes off. JC sees the cloak engage, paying attention this time. Fucking technology huh? He squints in the sunlight. Once the vessel is out of sight JC sees a couple scientists with digital clipboards standing outside of the landing platform. They wave at JC, who covers his eyes from the sun then waves back, adjusting his sunglasses. He notices two sexy assistants standing with them, he could get used to this. He approaches them casually as they wait eagerly to talk to their new specimen. A mini drone camera hovers alongside them, JC notices it at first then doesn't think much of it.

Heinrich, the German of the two scientists greets him first, 'good day to you, Mr Case. Hope your flight was pleasant, ja?' The drone circles them slowly.

JC is checking the girls out, 'it was OK, not bad for future (next-gen) tech.'

'Ah yes, future tech. Here we just refer to it as tech. (He chuckles to himself) The modern world is so clueless about the tech we have already since it is not on ze public market yet. Please if you follow me.'

The other scientist holds out his hand and speaks with an English accent, 'Dale's the name my boy. A pleasure to meet you.' A polite Brit as usual, JC thinks of the stereotypes, feeling like he's in a film, but isn't for once.

JC shakes his hand, 'no probs Doc.'

The scientists and girls walk off down the metal staircase and towards the main buildings and houses of the facility. The drone follows them all this time. JC is torn looking around at this magical surreal place and checking out the girl's behinds as they walk in front of him. The sexy assistants turn back and look to check him out and giggle. They reach the main buildings and one scientist veers off with his assistant and the other guides JC to his sleeping quarters. The drone flies off on another errand.

JC chucks his duffel bag onto the bed and looks around at his new spacious high tech bedroom. The flat also contains its own kitchen bathroom and living space. For a moment he remembers the show *Lost* and feels like this is a similar situation: lost literally. The scientist hovers by the door waiting for JC to turn around, his assistant peers over his shoulder.

'I hope ze facilities are to your liking.'

'I've seen worse on set.' Justin testing the waters of humour, if any.

The sexy assistant giggles realizing its sarcasm, but Heinrich doesn't get it at first. He looks at his assistant seeing that it was joke then attempts a fake/awkward laugh. JC makes eye contact with the assistant, who blushes. He then winks at the assistant. Heinrich, not too happy about this flirtatious behaviour speaks as he is about to shut the electronic sliding door.

'You will receive a tour of our lovely island tomorrow. Then we will begin testing the day after, yes?'

'Yeah whatever Herr Doktor, I can't wait.' The door slides shut with a spppppsshhhhhh sound. JC turns to his bag and starts unpacking. The rest of the night he spends eating some complimentary fruit having a shower and a shave. He opens the electronic closet door to reveal clothes supplied by the facility. He ignores the main clothes but notices t-shirts and socks. That night he reads about the island

and watches some demos describing the facilities on the high tech screen wall.

JC is woken up by a digital alarm he has never heard before, turns out it's one of the sexy assistants ringing the buzzer outside. As soon as JC gets up off his bed the blinds open automatically and his bed retracts into the wall. He is surprised by the speed of the tech in the room. He answers the security screen by the door. Lucy, one of the sexy assistant's faces can be seen.

'She's definitely a hottie,' he mumbles to himself.

'Um hello, Mr Case breakfast is ready to be served I will take you there now if you're dressed.'

JC presses a button on the screen, which turns out to be wrong one, it opens the door. JC is still in his boxers and topless. 'Uh shit sorry, I still need a manual for this door.'

Lucy giggles and blushes, 'I can show you myself later. How about for now you can get dressed and we will begin the day.' The same camera drone hovers behind her patiently, who knows whose watching or if it's even recording.

'Sure, give me a sec.'

'Sorry Mr-' the sexy assistant bites her lip as JC turns and gets dressed, he notices her watching him as he puts on his trousers. He looks up and she quickly shuts the door.

CHAPTER 8

DAY 1

They arrive in the mess hall, Lucy shows JC to the buffet filled with quality fruits, fresh made orange juice and instant coffee.

'Feel free to take your time eating. There is no rush here on the island.'

'Cool and thanks again (pause). What's your name?'

She is surprised since she does not tell many people her name.

'Lucille or you can call me Lucy.'

'OK Lucy, I'm Justin.'

'We all know who you are Mister Case.'

'Justin. Or you can call me JC, all my friends do.'

'Very well Justin. I'll be back in an hour.'

She walks off blushing worse than before. She has never met a living movie star before. All the celebrity inhabitants of the island are all clones of their previous selves. Once again JC checks out her behind as she walks off. He doesn't realize it now but she seems familiar somehow, as if possibly a celebrity once too. As he's thinking he gets distracted by the head Chef.

'You done with looking or you wanna order?'

JC is taken aback lost in his thoughts about Lucy. Some things don't change JC will always like girls.

Chef is an African-American stereotypical cook. However, he is a thinner version of Isaac Hayes in *South Park*.

'Sorry uh it's my first day here so still getting acquainted with the local-'

Chef cutting in, '-girls?'

'Um (pause) customs....'

Chef rolls his eyes, but then decides to play nice. He offers his hand, JC takes it slowly.

'You can call me chef, head chef, master chef. Whatever, as long as it's got chef in it. Clear?'

'Cool (pause) chef. So what's on offer today?'

'Same as every day, whatever you want. Pretty much anything you could wish for within reason that is.'

'K, how about eggs benedict.'

'Sure thing. Toast? Bacon?'

'Why not? You only live once right?' JC just realizes what he said and smirks at the situation. Chef chuckles. At least they're bonding now.

'Yeah right brutha.'

JC pours himself some orange juice and a coffee. He eats his meal alone in the massive space. He wonders how many staff really live here. Do they get to go home? Are they trapped here for good too? His food arrives and it tastes so good he forgets about all his previous thoughts. Afterwards he congratulates Chef on his cooking skills. They started off rocky but could be good living here after all.

Time passes and the sexy assistant reappears. 'The food to your liking?'

'Damn good. I tell ya. I'm loving this place already and what it has to offer,' saying this flirtatiously.

'Let's begin the tour shall we? We will start with a stroll on the beach then I will take you to where you will be working.'

'Working eh? That's what you call this place. More like a paid holiday if you ask me.' He follows her to the beach. On this occasion no drone follows them around.

Lucy leads JC around the island then to the main building which is located in the interior of the island, known as the Inner Sanctum. A large sign outside displays: GENETICS. She says goodbye for now and JC takes her hand and kisses it like in romantic French movies. JC enters the building leaving her love struck; she shakes her head and walks off. JC finds his way across a small lobby to one of the many science labs. All the rooms have glass walls so he can see into the individual rooms. There are just a few scientists besides the ones he already met.

He passes animal cages, high tech science equipment then comes to a room with Heinrich and Dale studying their microscopes and using touchscreen pads (like in *Avatar*) to confer with their data. They pass one of the pads back and forth not noticing JC standing behind a glass window watching them. He knocks gently and at first one of them hears him then the second. They swivel round on their chairs and walk to greet him. They both introduce themselves properly and then they sit down at the main (touch screen) table. Heinrich and Dale have their hands folded on the table with straight backs. JC slouches in his chair.

'I believe you have had breakfast and seen our beautiful island, yes?'

'Yeah it's a great place, but where are all the celebs I've been promised? I didn't just come to get cloned you know.'

'Patience. Please, Mr Case this is a top of the line high tech facility. They are constantly being tested and treated for various issues.'

'Issues you say, huh. I thought this cloning deal was obsolete. The best in the world I was told. How come I didn't see any in the canteen this morning?'

'They don't eat. They don't require nourishment. Helps keep everything cleaner don't u zink?' Heinrich thinking himself quite clever, having come up with that feature himself.

'If you don't feed em doesn't that contribute to their issues?'

'This is all very complicated; we don't expect you to understand this right away. This is simply a preliminary meeting you understand. The real work will start tomorrow.'

'What have I got to look forward to?' His eyes darting between the two scientists.

'We will begin wiz ze physical trials then ze mental ones. Collecting data you see.'

JC flexes his bicep, 'physical huh? Got no probs in that department.'

Dale taking a serious role, 'if you please Mr Case this is not a place to show off. You are not in Hollywood anymore. We are on the top of genetic engineering in the world.'

'K doc, I'm only playing. I just got one question.'

Heinrich takes an interest again, 'yez.'

'Is it gonna hurt?'

The two scientists look at each other, questioning whether to tell him the whole truth yet. They laugh awkwardly. 'We will build to zat. It is possible some of the procedures may be (pause) uncomfortable. But you are big strong man; you can handle zis, ja?' Mocking JC with his bicep move.

'If you say so Doc.'

Dale slaps the table gently, 'you will be an important part of history my boy.'

'Yeah but shame I had to get killed off for it.'

They all look a little sheepish, but then Heinrich decides to lighten the spirits. 'We have whiskey, very nice whiskey if you like. One drink zen we have to get back to work and you will come back tomorrow to begin properly. Wat do you zay?'

JC smiles, 'shit doc, now you talking my language.' The scientist pours 3 tumblers of aged whiskey, its top quality stuff. They clink their glasses and say together.

'Cheers!!!'

'One last thing Herr Doktor.'

The two scientists both look up at him if he's got something mindboggling intelligent to say.

'Could you uh hook me up with your assistant, Lucy I believe her name is?'

Heinrich bangs his glass on the table and snatches JC's empty glass off him.

'I got other questions too, like about the island itself.'

'We vill see you tomorrow Herr Case.'

Guess that ends introductions then.

That night JC sits alone on the beach gathering his thoughts. Did he make the right decision? Does he feel guilty about them faking his death so the whole world thinks he really was gone? What about his family? What about all the sexual conquests? And his sweet beautiful car, he will miss that too. As he is thinking about his Maserati, he notices a woman walking up the beach. He doesn't recognize her at first but once he hears her crying he stands up. Being the gentleman he is. She hasn't spotted him yet but he waits for her to come a bit closer. It's the sexy assistant, Lucy.

'Heh you there, Lucy right? You OK darlin?' He steps out of the shadows into the moonlight.

She quickly wipes away the tears and pretends like everything is normal. JC moves closer and wipes a tear off her cheek. She dips her head low as if ashamed. He lifts up her chin so they make eye contact again.

'Sorry I'm not supposed to see you anymore outside the lab.'

'What? Who made up that stupid rule?'

'My boss. He's the German scientist dealing with you.'

'Yeah, Heinrich. I know the one. How can I ever forget his accent? He sounds like he's from a bad B-Movie.'

Lucy giggles. She stands up straight and looks out to the sea then back at JC. 'Do you believe in fate Justin?'

'I didn't really before, but in a way I'm not sure anymore since I got dealt these cards.'

'Well, the Doctor doesn't want me to give you any more private tours or even spend any extra time with you.'

'I say to the hell with that! You're a grown woman. You can make your own choices right?'

'I guess, but I've never felt like this before.'

'Felt like what?'

'Attracted to someone,' she sheepishly looks at the ground.

'You mean like have feelings for. Hell, you must have experienced love before?'

'I was born on this island. I haven't lived on the mainland like you and the others. We live and work here, never allowed to leave.'

JC sweet talks her, 'well if it was up to me you could definitely leave anytime you wanted to.'

'Really? (Hopeful) It's all a dream anyways.' She turns to leave, but JC grabs her hand. He pulls her closer so they feel each-others breaths.

'Tell you what. I won't tell the Doc if you don't.' JC goes in for the kiss. She doesn't know what to expect since she's never been kissed before. She has her eyes open at first but then closes them as she gets into it.

CHAPTER 9
IT BEGINS

Inside the science lab over the next few weeks JC running with pads strapped to him, having his blood tested, X-rays, the works. He is like a hamster in a cage doing tricks for these older men. At one point when he is on the treadmill running he is topless with pads on his major muscle groups and a strap around his forehead. Lucy is there typing notes into the touch-screen computers and catches a glimpse of JC who smiles at her and winks. She blushes, and Heinrich notices this interaction. He stands in between them giving her a disapproving look. She turns away embarrassed, while JC sprints faster to show his great stamina.

Over time he continues with written exams and testing his IQ. Other tests include reaction times, speed, and agility. They even have a virtual simulation of a high tech war video game. This is probably his favourite test since it reminds him of the old army days, but without the danger part. The only difference now is his life isn't on the line, or is it? The two scientists are quite pleased with their healthy living specimen. One day, JC has enough of them stalling and brings up the question about the clones again.

'So Doctors, were getting to know each other, right? Sort of anyway, I still haven't seen any celebs running around. What's the deal?'

The doctors are evasive at first then Dale speaks up. 'Well you see, we have had them housebound since you arrived, but tomorrow we can release them once again. You will see.'

Justin sarcastically, 'can't wait.'

Later that night JC lies in his bed reading some book about cloning and genetics. He never had before, but decides he wants to learn about this place and the DNA process and hopefully truly understand it one day. His buzzer rings and he goes to open the door. The security cam is covered up by a hand.

'Uh, who is it?' Silence. He leans towards the door to try and hear anything that might give away the visitor. He opens up the door and Lucy is standing there.

'Surprise.' She is in a robe, which reveals nice lingerie underneath. JC is shocked how quickly she has come around, as if never having been with a man before. JC grabs her and pulls her inside, briefly peering outside to see if anyone was around. Still eerily quiet.

'What are you doing here? I thought you could get into serious trouble if we were caught.'

'I don't care about that anymore. I want you to be my first.'

'First? Hold on, you mean you're still a virgin?'

'I told you already I was born here and I am not allowed to be intimate with any of our subjects.'

'So what's changed?'

'You. You've changed me Justin. I've never cried before you appeared here. I never kissed anyone before you. And now I'm just, here.'

Justin sits them down on the bed, he's usually a playboy back home, but this place is weird. He's not as horny as he usually is; maybe it's suppressed by the island somehow.

'Wait. I just realized who you remind me of.'

'Who?'

Justin out loud, 'Lucille Ball. That's what you were called. I mean she was a bit before my time but I remember seeing her on the roast shows as a kid.'

'I'm sorry I don't know who or what that is.'

'It's a famous comedian show dating back decades. She was a famous actress/star from back in the day.'

'The doctors made comments about that lady once, he was chatting with the other doctor and I overheard them. Could it be I'm a?'

'Clone.' They have figured it out together; it did cross her mind from time to time.

Lucy places her head in her hands, 'oh no, I was never told that you mean I'm one of them, not human. Heinrich said I was special.' She starts crying again like that night on the beach. JC takes her hands in his and kisses her cheeks, tasting her tears. Even clones have salty tears. OMG.

'Heh, come now. It's not that bad (pause) being a clone. I mean you cry and you feel like any one of us. You might as well be human Lucy.' They make eye contact again and they mutually slowly move in for a kiss. JC isn't just using this woman, he actually feels for her too now. He's never been in love before either, come to think about it. There's a first time for everything I suppose. Early days still.

Outside JC's pad Heinrich is lighting up a cigarette under a palm tree. He lurks in the shadows. He squints his eyes, and then walks off back in the direction of his hut.

CHAPTER 10

LEGENDS

The next morning JC wakes up naked finding that Lucy has snuck out during the night. He smiles as he remembers flashes of her having an orgasm for the first time. Usually he has *experienced* girls in his beds. Never a virgin, of sorts.

Later JC enters the lab and sees Lucy working on a computer in the corner with her back turned. The two scientists are working on the touchscreen table looking at samples projected onto the wall monitors.

Justin happily chants, 'what's up my peeps?'

Lucy looks up briefly then back to her station. Heinrich barely moves deciding to ignore him. Dale unaware of the fling between JC and Lucy assumes everything is normal today like any other day. Except today, is the day they introduce JC to the other inhabitants.

'Ahh, Mr Case feeling refreshed are we?'

'Couldn't be better Doc. So what's on the agenda for today?'

'We have decided it's about time you meet the other inhabitants of this miracle island.'

'Cool, I was dreading another day being a hamster in a cage.'

The two scientists look at each other confused. He surely doesn't mean that their tests were redundant. 'Even better. Today you get to meet a legend.'

Justin leans in curiously, 'oh?'

'How would like to spar with none other than the dragon himself.'

JC can't believe his ears, 'no way. For real?'

'Yes, I think you are finally ready to make some new friends.'

Heinrich doesn't speak up during this period, he grumbles to himself from time to time. Maybe he is jealous that his new test subject is moving up in the world, on top of everything his dirty little secret with his assistant didn't help.

'You are talking about Bruce Lee right?'

'Precisely, follow me please. I will show you the banks first.'

'The banks?' JC frowns.

'You'll see.'

Further into the Inner Sanctum of the island, Dale and JC enter a large storage like warehouse; the temperature is below 10° Celsius or 50° Fahrenheit. The scientist helps himself to a warm coat and offers JC one. JC sweating from the sun outside declines then regrets it later. They pass through a pressurized glass door, a decontamination chamber. They enter the large structure which contains hundreds of clones being grown in glass containers. A viscous coloured fluid fills the cloned embryos vessels. There is a "pleasing to the eye" blue light accompanying each *test tube baby*. JC shivers at first, then really looks around marvelling at the space reaching up 2 stories and stretching for a while too. As he walks by containers, he spots names of famous people: Princess Diana, Michael Jackson, Bruce Lee, etc. They walk and talk.

'Shit, when I saw the video at CEU HQ I figured it was CG at first but now I really do believe my eyes.'

Dale confused, 'uh? CG?'

'A film term. Computer generated images.'

'So why don't they call it CGI?'

'They used to but they changed it, even the abbreviations get abbreviated in the business.'

'Sounds like the army.'

'Yeah quite similar actually. You're right. The core always said they enjoyed collaborating with film-makers cause of the hierarchy system.'

'I understand that perfectly.'

They continue walking past tube after tube of cloned embryos; they get larger towards the end where they are the size of small children. JC can recognize some features of the *bodies*.

'So tell me Doc, what's the deal with you and the other that Heinrich guy?'

'I don't follow.'

'Well is he the boss? Are you the boss?'

'Neither, he likes to think he's in charge but we have different backgrounds. He's German and I'm English so our countries have always had a bit of competition you know?'

'I served in two wars so I know, just not the ones you guys were in.'

'Heh, I'm not that old you know.'

JC laughs heartily. He puts his hand on the scientist's shoulder. The first camaraderie they've had alone. They exit the other end of the building into the blazing white hot sun.

On the west side of the island, JC and Dale come across a small temple with a Buddha overlooking a training platform looking out to the sea, surrounded by palm trees. For a second JC sees a glimpse of Asia somewhere especially once he hears those iconic screams. Bruce Lee is training by doing flips, kicks, and punches. He has a series of pots of various heights hanging from ropes attached to bamboo poles. He is topless wearing his traditional black pants. He does some roundhouse kicks then finally some high jumping kicks cracking every single one, most have water inside spraying everywhere. Some jars are filled with sand, for the punches. Bruce loves training even though a clay splinter cuts his knuckle. Like a scene from one of his films, he flexes his arm, then slowly lifts his hand to his mouth and licks it then thumbs his nose.

'Excuse me Mr Lee. I have the new arrival I would like you to meet.'

Bruce turns slowly with an intense look on his face at first, smiles and then he jogs over to them. Justin has to keep pinching himself to remind him that this is not a dream. He's faraway from *Kansas* now. They shake hands and Bruce and JC eye each other up and down. The scientist is smiling pleased for them to meet finally.

'How do you do?' The legend speaks.

'I'm fine thanks. It's an honour sir. I mean sorry you died and got brought back and everything.'

Bruce chuckles waving his hand, 'that's OK. What was your name again?'

'Yeah, um. Justin Case, I'm a movie star also. Well, I guess we were both stars once.'

'Well, at least I came back for a second life.' Bruce holds out his palm displaying the surroundings. JC marvels at his grace and the surroundings.

'It could be worse right?'

Dale joins the conversation again, 'I am so pleased you get along, well I'll take my absence now. Mr Lee, please try not to kill this one as well yes?'

Bruce rubs his nose again in his typical style, 'sure. No problem.'

JC looks concerned; he thought he was pretty tough but Bruce *the dragon* Lee that's a god among men. Bruce cracks his neck, and then waves JC to come over to the main platform.

Justin nervously, 'god it's so weird seeing you after watching all your movies. And-'

'And what?'

'After seeing your embryos just now.'

'Ah, he showed you those did he?'

'All I care about is that I finally get to see someone of your level. I studied martial arts too you know?'

'Jeet Kun Do?'

'Na sorry. I learned wing chun, kung fu and karate for some of my films.'

'That's good. How about a sparring match?'

'Awesome, no one inch punches OK?'

Bruce chuckles at this remark, as if he's got a surprise in store.

JC takes off his shirt revealing ripped muscles, his build is slightly larger than Bruce, but that doesn't matter when you're next to the god himself. His abs come close.

'OK, I'll try.' Bruce smirks.

JC is on his guard looking unsure if this is wise.

Bruce kicks fast high to the head.

JC blocks with his arms, but is amazed at the power knocking him to the side. His ears ring briefly. He may get a beating but this is a not your usual once in a lifetime experience. JC throws some punches, Bruce blocks every one. Even JC is surprised how quick he still is, despite the "you know what". Bruce and Justin go at it for a while until both are sweaty and bruised. JC is out of breath, Bruce is still fine. They take a break and chat some more.

'Not bad, but your footwork is lazy. Too slow I say.' With that famous accent of his.

'Coming from you I take that as a compliment. Mr Lee I just wanna say-'

'Please call me Bruce.'

'Wow, sure Bruce. It's pretty boring on the island so far. What do you do for fun round here?'

'Fun? No fun. Only train.'

'You mean there's no booze? No pills? No smoke?'

'You here to party or to work? This is no holiday.'

'I know. I'd just like to blow off some steam you know?'

'Steam? How about you train with me every day and I become your sifu?'

'Seriously? I would love that. I mean I don't know how much free time I have but I will check with the two Docs, see what they say.'

'Great. I have a new sparring partner and disciple.'

'Yes sifu. It's so cool that your here. I mean alive and well and all.'

'How about you come over to Di's house later we can chat some more?'

'Sorry who?' JC trying to imagine someone in his head.

'You know the ex-princess of England.'

'Oh you mean Lady Diana Princess of Wales?'

'Yeah, she having little house party. No alcohol. No drugs. OK?'

'That's cool. I'll be there.' Justin not knowing what to expect.

'You wanna train some more?'

Justin feeling his cracked ribs and bruises starting to form. 'That's OK Bruce. Not bad for a first introduction.'

'You can meet Brandon too if you come.'

'You mean Brandon, as in your son Brandon Lee?'

'The one and only.'

'Cool. I'll see you later.' JC bows (kow tow) and walks off slowly, limping. Bruce turns towards back to the sea and does some slow Tai Chi into the sun. It is later now so the sun is starting to go down; *magic hour* is beginning once again on the horizon. JC gets his shirt back on then realizing it is soaked in seconds. He has to get back and have another shower. This damn heat.

It gets darker as JC heads back to his pad, the islands network of lights come on one by one. He walks along the islands footpaths as he spots some of the other inhabitants. Pockets of celebrities cause JC's heart rate to rise and fall. He sees Bob Marley in the distance playing guitar with Kurt Cobain; they live close by each other. He stops briefly thinking if he should say hello. Then decides not to, there's still all the time in the world. He also doesn't want to intrude, plus he's still sweaty. It will take him some time getting used to this tropical heat.

CHAPTER 11

CLONE PARTY

Classic old style music is blasting out of the house. Before he enters the open doors, he marvels at the architecture of Diana's house. She definitely has the best looking pad out of all the celebs. JC enters looking like a tourist holding a map of the island in his hand. He did however shave and clean up. Brandon Lee is DJ'ing on a raised platform overlooking the dance floor. Bruce is sitting in a corner chatting to Elvis Presley. JC goes over in their direction when he spots Lady Diana shaking a cocktail shaker by her bar. JC can't wait, he decides to introduce himself.

'Uh excuse me, Miss Diana?'

Lady Di looks him up and down; she speaks in her traditional posh English voice. 'Why hello? You're quite the stunner aren't you?'

JC blubbering a bit, 'sorry to drop in like this but Bruce over there invited me.' They glance over at Bruce and Elvis, who give them a wave back.

'That's perfectly alright darling. Can I fix you a drink?'

'Bruce said there's no booze on the island. What have you got?'

She winks at him and smiles, 'well, what doesn't hurt him right?' Lady Di pulls out a secret cocktail shaker and makes a martini. JC takes it sipping it like a gentleman.

'Here I was thinking I'd never get any liquor for the rest of my life.'

'How ghastly that would be? There is a general rule: no toxins for the clones but I have a few contacts on the staff. Let me know your poison and I might be able to arrange something young chap.'

'That would save my ass,' in his typical comical American tone.

Lady Di laughs at the vulgarity then pours him a top up while she elegantly drinks from her glass. They flirt for a while; Bruce notices JC at the bar and tries to get his attention from across the room. JC doesn't want to leave the bar, but he must be friendly with all inhabitants obviously. He downs his drink, checks his breath, it seems to be clear. He waves bye to her blowing her a kiss as he walks off. JC walks past groups of old film stars including James Dean and Marilyn Monroe. He spots Brian Jones and Ian Curtis playing cards in the corner; he vaguely remembers their music but is still amazed. John Lennon and 2Pac Shakur are playing a game of pool on a table in a side room. He rubs his eyes just to check this still isn't a dream.

Bruce stands up and offers JC to sit down next to them. Elvis looks up at him.

'Justin. It's my pleasure to introduce you to-' Bruce gets cut off, from the one and only king of rock.

'-the King baby. You can call me Elvis if you like,' in his usual Southern drawl.

'Mr Presley, it's such an honour sir.'

'Cut the sir crap boy, your gettin me all shook up.'

'Oh my god, did you just really say that.' He can't believe his eyes or ears.

'What? Just trying to break the ice son.'

'Dude, like I can't believe I'm getting to meet you. My dad used to listen to your albums all the time when I was growing up.'

'Which ones? They ain't all that half bad you know?'

'I can't remember which. Such a long time ago.'

'You're pa sounds like a cool fella. What kinda music you like Justin?'

'Anything really. I saw Bob Marley and Kurt Cobain earlier tonight are they around?'

Elvis looks around the room, 'they're probably jamming somewheres.'

Justin addresses them both with his next question, 'sorry to be so up front with you guys, but do you know why everyone is being cloned in the first place?'

Elvis and Bruce look at each other unsure of the question. The King steps in. 'They tried to explain it once. In a seminar we were told something like cause we died under fifty or sumthin along those lines.'

Elvis replies, 'it's all good anyhow. We all living and have a second chance at life.'

'I'm still trying to figure this whole thing out. At first, I wasn't allowed to see anyone, I was getting real impatient.'

'That's right baby. Ain't nuthin but a hound dog.'

'Lol, you're funny you know that?' JC not thinking this is offensive.

'You gotta be in this place. I just wish they cloned some stand-up comedians for us entertainers and all.' Elvis lifts up his sunglasses looking JC directly into the eye, seeing if Justin got any comedy in him.

'I was an action star sorry, not a comedian.'

'Nothing to be sorry about bud. One more joins the party so to speak.'

JC confused by this but remembers that he is in the moment here and now with living dead celebrities. Elvis points towards the door. Just then Jimi Hendrix and Jim Morrison make some noise by the entrance. It's one hell of a party, Justin has rubbed shoulders with loads of living celebs but this took the cookie. JC looks over at the bar; Lady Di is entertaining JFK, Bobby Kennedy, Malcolm X and Martin Luther King Jr now. JC has lost his opportunity to romance her; she is way out of his league anyways.

The party carries on playing old classic tunes and some newer ones, JC slow dances with Marilyn Monroe later in the evening. She's another flirt though, too much competition she is easily distracted and floats between party guests. JC is in heaven though, surrounded by all these movie and music idols. Just then he sees the King of Pop and co chilling on a sofa together. MJ and Prince have got the shiniest and sparkly clothes out of anyone in this joint. He can't believe his luck, he is now friends with the majority of them. He is quite the talk of the party at first since he's a new arrival. Well his luck can't last forever.

An hour later JC walks outside the back to get a breath of fresh air, finding all these (dead) celebs in one place, it goes to his head a bit, spinning him out slightly. Outside chilling in the back garden are Kurt Cobain, Amy Winehouse, Paul Walker, Brittany Murphy, Heath Ledger and Ryan Dunn sitting around a campfire smoking a huge joint. Anton Yelchin joins them from the bushes after taken a leak; even clones need to go I guess. JC shyly walks over to their huddle and intrudes.

    Surprisingly JC is greeted by an enthusiastic crowd, 'heh, new guy!'

    'Um, sorry guys it was getting a bit crazy/wild in there.'

    Kurt Cobain in his deep voice calmly says, 'that's cool bra. Grab a seat if you like man.'

    Amy Winehouse follows Kurt with, 'yeah chill with us geez.'

    Justin feels respected and welcomed, 'thanks. You know I know you guys are clones and all, but–'

    Ryan Dunn cuts him off '–but you wondering if were even aware of our past (pause) real lives?'

    JC continues, 'I mean yeah. This whole situation is just so surreal you know?'

    Paul Walker takes a sip of American beer 'it's all good. Some of us were the same as you at first.'

    Justin curiously, 'same how? I'm still living.'

    A silence kicks in due to the inappropriate comment. Suddenly they all burst out laughing, JC feeling relieved he hasn't pissed them off, joins in the laughter too.

Paul continues, 'it's like this bro. We can't leave this place. Even if we wanted to, which we can't. I mean this place is paradise yo. Little slice of heaven.'

All the other clones in unison raise their drinks, 'I hear that.'

JC smiles knowing he's with good people, friends even. Anton is a bit shy still being one of the new additions to the island, he keeps to himself. Justin looks around and catches Amy checking him out. They make eye contact and she nods her head backwards to signal them to break away from the pack. JC spots this and signals with a nod in acknowledgment. Amy gets up and walks off by the bushes near the back of the garden.

'Can we pick this up later guys? I'll be right back.' JC sheepishly asks blatantly knowing that it is obvious why he's leaving the conversation. They all nod knowing exactly what's up. They checked that Amy left a minute prior. JC finds Amy hiding behind some palm tree/bush. When he spots her he slowly moves in close expecting her to kiss him right away, but instead she is sniffing some powder in the shadows. Looking up at him she offers him a line.

'Nah, I really shouldn't I'm gonna start training with Bruce tomorrow.'

She coax's it out of him. 'Oh come on mate; just have a little bump yeah.'

JC looks around checking no one followed them. He hasn't seen any camera drones at night, maybe they on charge somewhere on the island. Seeing the coast is all clear he leans in and snorts quick and hard. Amy chuckles as JC throws his head back. 'Man, wow. That's been a while.'

Amy giggles again. She puts away her *snorter* and coke box back into her handbag. Then she looks up at him looking all sexy with some moonlight streaked across his face. She gives him the look. They get closer to each other. Just before they kiss Amy breaks the silence. 'Wait, what was your name again new guy? Or I could keep calling you that if you fancy.'

'JC. Call me JC.'

Amy smirks, 'cool JC. I'm Amy.'

'I know who you were. I mean are.'

She giggles one last time biting her lip then pulls JC towards her and they snog for minutes. Turns out she's making the moves this time. The moon shines brightly in the night sky. He looks up as she kisses his neck. Upon closer inspection, JC notices the light of a massive dome, which surrounds the island, can be seen interacting with the earth's atmosphere. He'll question the Docs about that dome one day, if he remembers. It has a trippy feeling like a mini Northern Lights (Aurora Borealis).

At that moment he has a brain wave realising that all the clone's *ages* are from their prime as film and music stars. Not the old versions but when they were at the pinnacle of their careers. He has temporarily forgotten about Lucy, his new love and wrapped in someone else's lips for the time being.

CHAPTER 12

REVOLT

Some weeks pass and JC is back in the science lab again, Dale and Heinrich are analysing data like usual. Lucy is nowhere to be seen. JC has got his head down from lack of sleep and being quite hungover once again. Bad habit Justin, bad habit the old drink. Heinrich sneakily pricks him with a high-tech alcohol tester, which speaks out the results in seconds.

'Contents of person in question register high levels of alcohol in the blood stream results conclude unfit for driving or operating heavy machinery in all countries of the world.'

JC pulls himself up slowly realizing what the scientist just did. He opens his eyes slowly and looks around dazed.

'You know Herr Case alcohol is strictly forbidden on zis island for ze clones. Especially for all ze new test subjects.'

'Lucky I ain't one of em yet. Wait, is that what I am to you? Just another test subject?'

'Not exactly. You're our prime specimen, and we would like to keep you zat vay.'

'It was about time I mingled with the other inhabitant's right?'

'That's why I introduced you to Mr Lee.' Dale speaks up at last looking up from his digital pad.

'I'm still training with him, just partying on the side. It's not like it's gonna kill me or anything.'

Heinrich drills in the importance of his new life, 'can't you understand vat we are trying to do here Herr Case?'

'Take samples of me and then clone me I guess.'

Dale takes Heinrich's side, 'precisely. I have to agree with my lab partner here. It's better if you stay in shape and behave.'

'You mean no more going out at night?'

'No.'

'You mean not leaving my crib at all anymore except to come here every day and be bored?' JC asks this rhetorically.

'Precisely,' Heinrich says poshly.

Justin stands up too quickly losing his balance for a second due to the lack of brain cells, 'you mean I should just be a lab rat for you fucking wierdos!'

The scientists look at each other confounded by what they just heard. 'Mr Case if you please.' Dale tries to keep the room peaceful.

'Well, you guys have done enough tests on me for now! I'm done being pricked and prodded. And where the hell is Lucille?'

'You mean Lucy?' Dale asks innocently.

'Yeah Lucy, Lucille Ball. The famous actress!'

Heinrich snaps, 'I had her re-assigned!'

'What? Where? I wanna see her!'

'Impossible Herr Case.'

'Why? You know about us don't you?'

Heinrich looks away smugly 'I don't know vat you mean.'

Justin still standing, walks towards Heinrich with a mean look in his eye. The scientist feels threatened and backs up.

'I'm varning you Herr Case.'

'I'm warning you Herr Doctor. I'm gonna find out what's happening here. I wanna know what you did to her.'

Dale pleads, 'Justin please stop this behaviour!'

JC snaps his head towards Dale, 'Justin is it now? What happened to Mr Case this, Herr Case that?'

'Please! We don't vant to but vill if forced.'

'And do what exactly? Huh?'

Dale trying his bluff, 'we do have security on this island you know.'

'Yeah where? I haven't seen any since I arrived. All I've seen is those damn drones followin me around all the time.'

'Never mind the drones; they're all the security we need. The mainland is only alerted when an emergency arises.'

'Is this not an emergency Doc? You know I'm done with all this Mickey Mouse bullshit! You guys and your good cop bad cop routine. I'm outta here.'

Heinrich reaches into his coat pocket, 'don't make yourself regret zis you can still apologize. It's not too late.'

JC storms towards the exit. 'Fuck this!' Just as he is about to exit the glass swivel doors, he feels a prick in his back. At first he's in shock not knowing what hit him, he tries to reach around but can't pull the dart out. Heinrich is holding a tranquilizer gun still aiming at Justin. JC has fallen slouched up against the glass doors, his face sliding down the glass. Making a screeching noise all the way down.

Dale grabs the tranquilizer gun from the Heinrich's hands. 'What the bloody hell are you doing?'

'Protecting myself from zat maniac!'

'He was probably gonna sleep off his aggression. He was blatantly still drunk from last night.'

'I zink he should be locked up for a while. Let him detox'

'Well we may not have a chance in hell now. We could just put him back in his room and hope he won't notice he's been drugged.'

'Hope? Vat hope? He is a menace and needs to learn discipline.'

'Very well. And why was he getting so upset when you said you sent Lucy away?'

'Lucy and him became (pause) shall we zay involved.'

'And what of it?'

'She vaz mine. And mine alone to keep. Not his.'

'We're going to have to clone another one!'

'I have a better idea. Let's lock zem up togezer.'

Dale shocked, 'you mean she's still alive? Good god man. What did you do with her?'

'After having my fun wiz her, I locked her up in ze jail cell.'

'You are a twisted and sick man Heinrich. Did I ever tell you that?'

Heinrich taking this as a compliment instead as an insult, 'not until now.' Chuckling to himself.

'Well, let's deal with him and get back to our research.'

'Agreed partner.' They go over to JC, lift him by the armpits and drag him out.

In an *old tech* dark prison cell JC wakes up with a killer headache. He remembers flashes of the science lab, some shouting. Then, being shot in the back by a dart. He leans up fast and confused about this new dark place he finds himself in.

'What the fuck! Where the hell am I?'

A shuffling is heard in the next cell and then a voice speaks quietly. 'Justin? Thank god you're finally awake?'

JC looks around, he can't see very much yet but his eyes adjust within seconds. They are in two cells in a dingy part of the island, probably underground. A tiny shaft of light shines through some top window in the hall. He notices he's in a metal cage like structure: aka a *low budget* prison cell. He reaches out the bars hoping to find Lucy's hands.

'Lucy, baby. Are you OK?' Their hands touch and their fingers intertwine.

'I'm doing OK I guess. Heinrich locked me in here just yesterday.'

'Did he say why?'

'He was pissed at us, I tell ya. Jeez. He drugged me and I think he even raped me.'

'What? That mother fucker! I'm gonna kill him!'

'I mean he did create me and everything, but it was nothing like you were though.'

'Lucy. I know you're just a clone and all but you gotta know nowadays a woman has a right to say no. This isn't the 50's anymore.'

'Oh OK. If you say so darling. So what's the plan? Are we gonna get outta here?'

'I don't know. I just don't.' JC wrestles with the metal bars, they don't budge. He paces around his cell for a while. Then he tries some questions. 'When did Herr Doctor last come and visit?'

'When he dropped you off here I guess. Am I being punished because I'm a woman or a clone?'

'He's just jealous of what we got.'

'What have we got Justin?'

'Love baby girl. Love.'

Lucy blushing alone in her cell, 'you mean that. Really?'

Justin sensing it before but truly believing it now, 'sure I do. Listen here's what we're gonna do.'

The following morning JC and Lucy are both asleep in their cells when Heinrich comes in and wakes them up with lights coming on and banging of some kind.

'Vake up sleepy heads. I have a shot for our non-clone and no shot of life for our clone.' He stares them both down feeling the power of having the upper hand. They may die in here, they may not. The future is uncertain.

JC slowly gets up and approaches the bars. 'Listen Heinrich is it? We got off to a bad foot here. So why don't we start from scratch again OK?'

Heinrich is intrigued by this change in behaviour but does not trust it; Justin was an actor after all. He leans in with an eyebrow raised. 'Zat may be Herr Case. However I want zis to be a lesson to both of you. You are not free to run around as you please. You signed your life away and once you are successfully cloned you are expendable. Do you understand?'

JC decides to play nice. 'Yeah sure doc, whatever you say. Heh you the boss, right? I was hung over I didn't mean anything by it, OK?'

Heinrich pulls the keys out of his pocket dangling them in front of him. For a moment it looks like JC is gonna be freed. But then Heinrich starts laughing sadistically. He throws his head back enjoying this power battle.

'You thought it would be zat easy did you? You can't fool me Herr big Movie Star.'

JC stops pretending and reaches out for Heinrich; he barely grabs his lab coat lapel. All he manages is to grab a pen from the Doctor's breast pocket. 'You fucker. I'm gonna get you. You bastard! Lucy told me what you did to her!'

'I don't zink so Herr Case. Not today anyvay.' Heinrich pulls out the tranquilizer gun again and aims it at JC's head. JC ducks and dives around his cell using a pillow to block the shot. Heinrich laughs some more as he keeps aiming for a clear shot. Eventually he gets lucky and shoots JC in the leg. JC immediately drops the pillow and looks down; he manages to pull it out. It is too late within 3 seconds he's out again.

JC wakes up for the second time with a killer head ache. He is on the floor at first; so he stumbles to his feet reaching around in the dark. He calls out.

'Lucy! Lucille you there?' Silence. 'Fuck, she's gone. Now what?'

He steps on the pen from the doctor, which was still on the floor. He remembers training for a film role where he had to learn how to pick locks. He takes the pen apart and combines the centre ink section with a bed spring and builds a makeshift key. After fiddling with the primitive lock for a minute he manages to open the cell door. Finally, some luck.

He slips out of the corridor, which reveals another hallway. He sees pictures and etchings in the walls of past celebs that caused trouble and were locked up here. He even finds some folders, reading through early test subjects reactions to the cloning. Some incidents date back to the mid 1900's.

A case file notes that: the test subject became increasingly violent and incarcerated at first, but after a month the subject was unresponsive to treatment then destroyed. JC looks up and around and sees boxes of folders dating up to 10 years ago. He wonders why they stopped. Maybe the treatments finally worked. He keeps a page from the folder he was reading: *just in case.*

It is night time and JC sneaks around from shadow to shadow avoiding the main footpaths that are lit up. He decides he's had enough of this place. He's got a plan how to deal with the scientists but not yet of how to get off the island. He needs to interrogate the two doctors first.

He packs his clothes and personal items in case he does get off the island in one piece. He leaves the books on cloning even chucking them on the floor. Damn island and its rules.

JC breaks in by simply sneaking in through an open window. Heinrich is in bed sleeping, while Lucy is tied up on the floor in the corner. JC sneaks over to Lucy and gently wakes her up. She has bruises on her face and her make-up, a mess due to the tears and smudged mascara. He holds his finger over his lips as he begins to untie her. He hears Heinrich tossing onto his back, so JC freezes but relaxes when he hears snoring. He finishes untying Lucy then goes over to the bed. He stands over Heinrich, who is still on his side. JC blocks the moonlight coming in through the window then leans down and starts blowing on Heinrich's face to wake him up. Heinrich still in REM wakes up startled and confused thinking he might still be dreaming. JC shoves his hand on Heinrich's face covering his mouth.

'Don't scream and I won't have to knock you out!' As JC takes his hand away Heinrich attempts a plea for help, but is quickly silenced when JC punches him in the face, knocking him out.

'Told ya.'

It is late that very same night Heinrich wakes up gagged and groggy, he winces at the pain from the side of his head. He opens his eyes and looks around. They are in the science lab and Dale is tied up next to him already awake and looking at him with tired eyes. JC and Lucy are sitting opposite on one of the counters, they are kissing passionately. Heinrich and Dale both being gagged attempt a few mmmmm's to get Justin's attention. JC and Lucy notice the commotion and take a break from smooching.

'Ah look who's finally awake. Cat got your tongue Herr Doctor?' JC hops off the counter and pulls off the two gags. Heinrich is wriggling around trying to break free. Dale keeps quiet, not wanting to escalate this situation.

'Herr Case, you vont get away wit zis. Untie us now and we can go back to normal ja?'

'I don't think so Doc. Problem is, you locked me up for being drunk. And shot me twice.'

'And disorderly,' Dale whispers.

JC gives him a quick look then back to Heinrich. Dale looks away not wanting to cause more trouble than they are already in.

'As I was saying, the problem is this. Lucy and I want off this place. Anywhere but here stuck with you two.'

'Out of ze question! You are top secret scientific experiment; you signed your life away. Even if you did get off zis island, zay would hunt you down to keep zer national security secret.'

'Well I stopped giving a shit OK. And Lucy is done being your sex slave, got it?'

Dale gives Heinrich a dirty look. 'Again? You didn't, did you Heinrich?'

Heinrich shrugs it off, 'psssfffffttt.' He looks away from Dale.

JC kills the moment getting on with his plan, 'one of you is gonna help me I don't care which one, but I will get off this island one way or the other.'

'This is a top secret facility; zer is no way off of here.'

'So what you're telling me is that you two are stuck here for good too.'

'Not exactly,' Dale speaks up.

Heinrich quickly snaps his head to give Dale the evil eye. 'Don't you dare!'

JC ignores the unruly German, 'go on Doc.'

'If you remember your arrival, you landed specifically at a certain time yes?'

'The time storm?'

'Indeed.'

'Of course, how could I forget? They said they only arrive at a certain time because of the Bermuda triangle time portal. So when's the next delivery?'

'Don't you tell zem a zing, Dale!'

JC smacks Heinrich hard in the face with his back hand. Lucy comes over and starts pushing her foot against Heinrich's crotch. He winces in pain from both injuries.

Dale scared seeing this, 'I'll help you if you take me with you.'

'Dunno about taking you with us, but you sure can help.'

'Anything I can do to convince you. I'm on your side. I'm done defending Heinrich from now on. He is a filthy pig with no human morals.' He catches a glimpse of recognition from Lucy.

JC looks between Dale and Heinrich. His eyes suggest a possible plan to kill Heinrich. JC winks at Lucy, then nods for Dale's restraints to be taken off. Lucy goes round the back and starts untying Dale's rope. Heinrich is becoming more restless again. He starts struggling and panicking as he realizes what the next step is.

'You can't do zis to me! I'm am head researcher of zis facility! What of all the clones! Zay will all die even your precious Lucy.'

JC looks concerned, he signals Lucy to stop untying Dale. 'What's he talking about Doc?'

'He means the medication they must take or else.'

'Medication? What meds? I thought you said they don't eat.'

'They don't eat; it's an enzyme deficiency booster. They need it once a month or else their cloned cells start dying. We only produce this medicine here on the island.'

'Well can't we just take them with us?'

'There's enough here to last for decades, but how are we gonna transport it? It would only be for Lucy in this case. So we could take some supplies, but if they are not re-manufactured she will die eventually.'

JC and Lucy look at each other with concern. 'Is that all doc?'

Heinrich sees his opportunity, 'I could help you wiz ze formula if u let me go. Not him.'

JC paces thinking of what to do next. Dale is trying harder to stay alive.

'Bollocks. I have the formula. He doesn't.'

'No I do. You have part of ze formula not ze whole massematical equation.'

Justin rationalises, 'kay, you both bought your ticket to stay alive a bit longer. Dale, are there any weapons on the island?'

'You mean besides the tranquilizer gun? Unfortunately not.'

'I thought you said there was some type security here, don't they have weapons?'

'What security? You believed that? (laughs) We are virtually cut off from the world. We have drone cameras linked to one automated security office. We don't need any more prying eyes around here. This place is for our eyes only'

'OK, how about if we shut down those drone camera thingy's first, and then send out an SOS call to the main land.'

'SOS. Ha! We have no permanent contact wiz anybody. Only once a month the supply chopper arrives to drop off equipment and or passengers such as yourself.'

'So when is the next shipment due?'

Dale confesses all, 'next week.'

'OK so we just have to sit tight till the bird arrives then sabotage it somehow.'

Heinrich snorts, 'sabotage. Pffftttt. You won't last von second.'

'You leave that up to me doc.' JC knocks out Heinrich again.

JC and Dale head to the security centre first and install a loop video surveillance program. At the same time shutting down all the drone cameras simultaneously, without alerting the mainland.

Then after several hours of scraping together ingredients for homemade plastic explosive from various cleaning products JC is making some explosives with Dales help. He sweats as JC is taking it in his stride. He's never made bombs before.

Once complete they strap the homemade plastic explosive against every other tank to at least explode most of the pods containing growing fake celebrities.

JC spots a back room sealed with a vault like door. As he enters he is shocked by cloned politicians from around the modern world. At first he doesn't recognize them, but upon a closer look he recognizes a previous president of the USA: Barack Obama. Then he sees others including Bush senior & junior even potential candidates like Hillary Clinton and Donald Trump. He can't believe his eyes. These clones were definitely not parading around the island. He calls Dale over from outside the vault door.

'Shit Doc is this for real?'

Dale embarrassed, 'I'm afraid so, this is all highly top secret remember. This is the very reason why Heinrich didn't want you snooping around on your own.'

Justin is amazed, 'no shit! Oh this place is going down brother. After we blow this thing let's gather the rest of the clones and tell them the whole truth about this place and how they could die once we leave this place.'

'I agree, but what if they become (pause) aggressive? We've had incidents in the past.'

'A saw some files back in the dungeon. We can use that aggression to get off this joint. They can help with the chopper.'

'But you won't be able to take any of them with, you do understand?'

'I'm only taking one clone as proof, and-'

'For love?'

'That's right doc. We can take some of that serum you boys go on about. You know, the one that keeps their cells from-'

'Breaking down and collapsing on a molecular level.'

'Sumthin like that.'

'We make quite the team, eh?' Dale seeks recognition.

'Cool your horses Doc, we ain't off this rock yet. That about does it.'

They stand back and marvel at the cabling going from tank to tank connecting the homemade plastic explosive. Dale hands JC the homemade detonator carefully. It is not yet switched on but they wouldn't want any accidents before departure.

JC and Dale stand outside the facility *just in case* the whole of the inside is blown out. JC flicks the on switch; a red light appears on the detonator.

'Here she blows.'

Just before he pushes the button, Dale chips in last minute. 'Are you sure we have enough explosives?'

'Should do, I learned this shit during my military training.'

'Like most of your skills I keep hearing about.'

JC gives him a nod. Dale puts his fingers in his ears. JC flicks the switch and flinches, nothing happens immediately. Then after a three second delay, they have not only blown up the whole of the inside of the structure, but the blast wave causes the glass doors at the front and back to blow outwards. This sends glass flying their way, so they duck down luckily a safe distance away. The explosion makes the sound of a bomb in a confined space, yet the roof is blown out and creates a massive cloud of black smoke rising. JC starts laughing, Dale smirks unsure of how to react, with joy or fear. Once they get up JC smacks Dale on his back hard, Dale flinches. They brush off debris and dirt from their clothes and faces. They are both covered in dust particles.

'We did it Doc! Wasn't sure that would work for sure.'

'It seems to have done the trick sir,' Dale says having a new found respect for JC.

A commotion is heard behind them as more and more clones join the show having never witnessed anything like this before. They marvel at how the smoke is darkening the sky and blocking the blaring sun. They cover the top of their eyes with their hands (e.g. Lady Di), others simply put on their sunglasses (members of 27 Club). Some approach JC and Dale looking for answers of this disturbingly loud noise and polluting smoke. Some of the smoke collects in the top part of the islands dome.

Kurt Cobain speaks up first, 'bra, what's going on here man? I was having my afternoon snooze and then boom.'

Bob Marley scratching his dreads, 'ya mon, me burn me-self on my spliff mon.'

JC turns to them individual, 'quiet down my friends. I can explain everything. Let's gather in the mess hall and I mean everyone (looking at his watch) in an hour. Cool?'

Even Ryan Dunn is pissed at him despite the bonding on all the nights prior, 'dude this better be a good damn explanation bro.'

'It will blow your mind.' JC says whilst still brushing off debris from his clothes and hair.

'Cool man. See you there.'

JC gives Dale a last look. 'We gotta get Heinrich; he will put on one hell of a show.'

'Not sure he can top that one Mr Case,' Dale squeezes JC's shoulder.

JC smirks as they head back to the lab where Lucy has been keeping Heinrich *company.*

CHAPTER 13

THE PLAN

All the island's inhabitants are gathering in the mess hall curious to find out what JC was up to blowing up the cloning facility. JC is not there yet but they all wait murmuring to each other about possible scenarios. All the musicians/rockers (27 Club) are together, all the politicians with their group. MJ, Prince and 2PAC huddle together guessing what all this is about. Even Bruce Lee is sitting with his son Brandon.

Heinrich is still gagged and strapped to a chair as he gets wheeled in by the side entrance by Lucy. Then Dale follows close behind and finally JC. A rabble breaks out, people shouting for answers, JC cool as ever holds up his hands and calms the crowd down. He looks around at all *his new friends* and begins his speech.

'I know you all got questions and up until yesterday even I didn't have the answers. Well look here people; a great fraud is being committed on this island.'

Ryan Dunn shouts out, 'no shit bro!' Referring to the commotion from earlier.

Most of the clones laugh, some don't find it so amusing. Heinrich struggles in his chair with his restraints and gag.

Justin continues his speech, 'listen the truth is when I first found out about this place, I didn't believe it. I couldn't fathom the magnitude of this magical place. I was too busy getting famous and rich on my own terms. As we all here know being a celebrity isn't always that easy.'

The crowd add some, 'hmmmm hmmmmss' and nod in agreement. As if in a church and JC is the preacher.

'That said. I have never imagined my dream would be to live and know all of you great famous dead stars. Some of you have become my friends some I have even partied hard with.' A few laughs in the audience.

'But know this, I have uncovered a dirty secret and this is why none of us are ever allowed to leave this island.'

Kurt Cobain speaks up, 'what is it bra?'

Amy Winehouse is curious too now, 'tell us more mate. What is this big secret you on about?'

'I'm getting to that Amy, you look great today by the way.' Amy blushes, JC smirks and winks at her, hoping Lucy didn't catch that. 'Cheers darling.'

Lucy standing behind JC squints her eyes at Amy, saying he's mine you - back off.

'K here it is. These doctors you've met and been treated by have undertaken the conspiracy of all conspiracies. Not only cloning all of you probably more than once but modern leaders as well.' Murmurs around the hall.

Brandon Lee joins in too now, 'what's that got to do with us and this place?'

'They are committing a crime so grave that living as a human seems immoral altogether. That's how this place gets its funding; they sell clones to anyone that can afford it. They are placing these puppets around the world in place of real people.'

'So?'

'So, Brandon, that means the public have a right to know they are being cheated. They have the right to know they're voting for impostors. Clones! No offence to Lady Di, JFK, and company. You're all dead so that doesn't apply to you guys anymore. However, if the world found out about you all, we could possibly remove the government and there could be absolute anarchy.'

Kurt speaks up again, 'I'm all for anarchy but how can we help? We can't just leave here. Can we?'

Justin looks down having to explain the plan, 'no Kurt, you can't, not yet anyway. But I can and will come back for you. However, I'll need your help first. All of you in fact. You will have enough serum to live another few months. Hopefully by then I could convince the world that you guys are real people and not just cloned copies of the original celebrities.'

Lady Di sees the injustice knowing corruption from her living days, 'how can we help luv?'

'I have a plan, the next chopper is arriving in 2 days from now, and we can form units of distraction. It is going to be a giant magic trick of epic proportions.'

All the clones lean in as JC lays out his plan of attack. They will rehearse it like a scene for the next two days until they have it perfect.

CHAPTER 14

ESCAPE

Two days later. Dale is waiting with Lucy by the helipad and his usual clipboard in hand. All the celebrity clones are waiting by the mess hall and some hiding in the bushes. JC, Bruce & Brandon are nowhere to be seen. A loud boom is heard as the chopper/jet crashes through the time barrier and for the first time, some of the clones can see it appearing through the dome like structure high up in the clouds. It approaches in silent mode outside the *the dome*, but once inside it hovers before descending which gives off its general location. One can only see the cloaking feature of the aircraft when it passes in front of the clouds, then it switches to *vision mode*. The black silhouette descends beginning its landing protocol.

Inside the cockpit the pilot and co-pilot communicate with each other, 'all checks are good for landing with a scan of the wind conditions favourable. Commencing approach.'

The co-pilot peers through a window hatch, 'I don't see the second doctor, usually he's always with. Oh well, maybe he's sick or something.'

'Landing vectors approved. Commencing landing.'

'Roger that.'

The craft lands slowly and smoothly this time round, like true professionals they touch down without a hitch. The rotor engines slow down as it revs down to stand-by mode. The Co-pilot opens the side door and begins delivery of some foods and spare medicine for the humans inhabiting *celebrity island*. Dale and Lucy walk up to the craft and start piling up the boxes as if nothing out of the ordinary is going on.

'The other Doc sick today?' The co-pilot asks casually.

Dale acts his heart out trying to pretend nothing is wrong, 'yes, he has a bit of a stomach bug you see.'

The co-pilot continues passing medical boxes to Lucy. 'Nasty. Well the usual delivery of meds and food stocks.'

'Excellent.' Dale, awkwardly imitating Mr Burns from *The Simpsons*, continues his checklist on his digital pad.

Then a mass wave of clones start appearing by the tree line and coming from the mess hall. The co-pilot doesn't notice at first but having his wireless headset on he is still in communication with the pilot.

'What the fuck? You seein this?'

'What?' The co-pilot looks up and spots the movement of all the inhabitants approaching. They all begin to clap loudly as if applauding after a show.

'Something's up. Get ready to get your ass back in here.'

'They probably just wanted to watch us arrive for once; they never get to in their schedule I mean.'

'That's why I'm gettin twitchy. I got a weird feeling here.'

'You sure? Seems like normal, the Doc's here signing for the goods. We'll be outta here in a sec. Just a couple more boxes.'

Underneath the raised helipad, JC is waiting with his backpack, Bruce Lee in his famous yellow outfit and Brandon dressed as the crow. Together they leap up onto the platform and charge the co-pilot and the chopper. The co-pilot with his back towards them doesn't spot the silent attack. He gets pinned to the floor by the *two dragons* as JC grabs a tazer off of him. Then Justin runs for the open hatch.

Before the pilot can react to his partner being taken out, JC is in the chopper with him and has the tazer aimed right at his head.

'You can't do this! You know the rules! You can't ever leave this place!' The pilot pleads.

'Those rules can kiss my ass! You taking us back to the mainland or I'm gonna shoot you in the face with this here tazer which should about kill ya within seconds.'

The pilot cockily, 'it's only a Tazer that ain't no real gun.'

'You wanna risk a direct shot to the face? We can find out if you like and I can try pilot this here chopper myself.'

'You? Ha! You're just a movie actor! This is a high-tech state of the art vehicle. You couldn't navigate through the time displacement portal!'

'I flew a couple hueys back in the day. Anyways, I'd rather die trying then live out the end of my days in this place.' JC wedges the Tazer right under the pilot's chin and forces it upwards.

The pilot finally gives in. 'OK fine, when we get back, you're gonna have the whole world on your ass!'

'I'll take my chances. Lucy, Doc we good to go!' Dale and Lucy jump aboard and strap themselves into their seats. Dale and Lucy look back at Bruce and Brandon standing holding the co-pilot. The craft begins to kick its engines back into gear. The revs get louder temporarily once more. Bruce, Brandon and the co-pilot back off slowly.

JC hops into the co-pilot's seat and puts on a spare headset and talks through the mic first to the pilot second through the megaphone attached to the front of the craft.

'I'm watching your path Major. You take us anywhere besides where I wanna go, you gonna find out how many volts your brain can take before meltdown, you dig?'

The pilot adamantly, 'I already told you I would get you back, after that your fate is doomed.'

Justin's patience has run out, 'shut the fuck up and fly already. Take off.'

The engines are ready for lift-off and it slowly takes off a few metres at first, then the engines are back in stealth mode and he can address his crowd. The craft is unheard but his voice echoes around that part of the island. JC talks to the celebs left on the ground, as he mentions each person they look up and smile when they hear their names.

'My fellow celebrities. I thank you all for helping me accomplish this feat. I couldn't have done it without you all. Diana, thanks for your hospitality and cocktails. Chef, keep cooking those amazing breakfasts. Kurt, Amy, and the rest of 27 Club keep chilling. Bob, you still my hero. Ryan, Paul and Anton you died way too young. I promise I'll come back and get you all. Elvis, you always be da king baby. Marilyn, you're gorgeous and you never did need all those pills. The rest of you I'll miss ya and I promise I'll die trying to expose this secret place and bring you all back home, back into the public light. Finally, my hero Bruce and your son Brandon, you two dragons will live forever in my heart and mind. Keep training until I come back and we can spar again soon. Stay alive and I'll be back as soon as I can.'

The craft turns and faces the dome and the clouds; the cloak is fully engaged now. The celebs are squinting looking up high in the sky, barely being able to follow the invisible crafts trajectory. They begin waving and cheering, for most of them JC was a new spice in their lives. He brought something new to the island; they would each remember the times they shared with him and the laughs they had. Months passed but he had changed their boring lives forever. Maybe he was never meant to be caged for the rest of his life. He still had a choice, they didn't. All they knew now was this *lost island*. They were happy for him to make it off this place when escape seemed impossible.

From bright sunny day they cross over the time displacement barrier and it is night time all of a sudden. Something is going wrong, the craft is shaking violently, and sparks shoot out of the panels. The inhabitants of the craft are panicking and shouting at each other.

'What the hell is going on?' Justin screams.

'Remember when I told you that time teleportation is not perfect and can glitch from time to time!'

'Yeah why?'

'This is one of those times!'

'You best not be trying to sabotage this here operation Major!'

'Why would I try and fuck this up? I could die too you know!'

'Just land this thing as safe as you can!'

The pilot is struggling with the controls and the joystick/steering wheel, which shudders violently. 'We're still over the ocean! What the hell you think I'm trying to do?'

A loud bleeping is heard and a flashing red light fills the whole craft. It is the warning noise that the engines are failing and the craft is descending rapidly. Even the cloak is disengaged now.

'Hold on tight! We goin down!'

JC, Dale, and Lucy tighten their straps and grab onto their seats any way they can. The craft is shaking even more now and their fear and paranoia of crashing increases every second due to the fast downward acceleration. The pilot sees a large transport ship and heads towards it.

Somewhere in the Atlantic they smash, hit the sea, first diving under water like a sea bird then levelling out on the surface. A silence fills the cockpit first, and then within the minute the passengers start coming to one by one. The front window is cracked badly and sea water is squeezing through the cracks. As JC comes to he feels the whiplash in his neck, rubbing it in pain. Lucy has a cut on the side of her head and blood is dripping from her hair. Dale wakes up groggily and begins undoing his then her safety belt/straps. JC calls out.

'Doc! Lucy! You guys OK?'

Dale speaks for the both of them while Lucy is still coming to, 'we're OK, and you?'

JC rubs his whiplashed neck, 'fucked my neck up but I'll live. Major? Major! You still with us?'

Silence. JC gets out of his chair and looks into the cockpit. The pilot is slumped over forwards and is bleeding from the front and back of his head; he is unconscious still or dead. JC checks his pulse; he tries first on the neck then the wrist. Nothing. JC rubs his head and hair. He looks through the window and spots the leak then a massive cargo ship. A loud ship horn blares out. He goes round the side and opens the hatch, struggling at first to get it open. At least the craft is floating and not sinking. JC spots a flare gun on the side by the door panel.

He climbs on top of the vessel and fires a flare into the sky. No reaction from the Chinese cargo ship as it sails away. He fires another shot directly towards the massive ship's cockpit/bridge. It narrowly misses, and then a loud ship horn is heard once more. Luckily the ship slows down and search lights begin panning around the sides and back. Eventually a search light illuminates JC and the floating craft, he starts waving and shouting like a madman even jumping up and down, to make sure they are not stranded. He calls down into the cabin.

'We OK y'all! We gonna be rescued no worries.'

Dale is holding Lucy who is shivering next to him. 'Lucy needs to see a doctor ASAP or if we have access to a first aid kit I can patch her up.'

'That's good Doc, keep her warm for me. (Jokingly) Don't get any ideas.'

Dale shakes his head and takes his lab coat off and wraps it around her shoulders.

They are inside the massive Chinese container ship JC, Dale and Lucy are wrapped up in space blankets and a female Chinese medic Xiaou is seeing to Lucy's wound on the side of her head. They are all on cots crammed into a small room. Dale and JC are drinking warm cups of tea.

'Heh Miss Doctor lady. Where you say we docking again?'

In her broken English, 'Los Angeles port.'

'You let us know when we close we gonna take a shortcut off this boat. Can you guys spare a dinghy?'

'No understand. You must go customs.' She assumes he's kidding shrugging her shoulders.

'Whatever you say Doc, just let us know OK?'

'Sure. No problem.' The medic applies a bandage to Lucy's head after cleaning the wound. She writes in a clipboard and walks to the door. 'You rest now OK. I come back later check on you.'

She dims the lights. They all lie back down and talk more about the *new* plan of arrival.

'We can't go through customs, you guys know that much. So here's what we'll do.'

CHAPTER 15

RETURN

Back on mainland in a phone booth, JC makes a desperate phone call to his one and only (ex) agent. It rains during the whole conversation. The phone rings for a while until finally an answer.

'Tom Wilkins speaking.'

'Tom, it's me.'

'Me who?'

'Justin.'

Tom is about to put down the phone, 'is this some kind of prank, Justin Case died in a car crash half a year ago. I don't find this amusing whoever you are.'

'K, remember at your wedding I slept with all the bridesmaids except one, only you and I would know her name.'

'Go on. You get this right and we can talk.'

'Samantha.'

'Last name?'

'Jennings. I got your attention now?'

'JC what the fuck? Is it really you, I mean you were my best star and then one day you were gone just like that. If you're not dead, what the hell where you doing all this time?'

'It's a long story, but I'm back but gotta stay under the radar if you know what I mean.'

'I'm listening. What do you need? A car? A pad?'

'It's more complicated than that. I have something that will blow this whole country away.'

'Another movie, let's talk dollar signs. Any figure.'

'Just hear me out OK?'

'Sorry, it's just I can't believe it's really you and your back. Old habits die hard.'

'Shut up and listen. Do you still have your contacts in the secret underground news network?'

'Jenny and Hector?' Tom scratches his head remembering his old college buddies.

'Whoever they were. I remember you chatting about them once at a meeting. Can you get me in contact with them for me?'

'Sure. I mean I haven't spoken to them in a while since you're uh (pause) death. They always thought it was a conspiracy.'

'Great I'm hiding out for now can I call you back in an hour and have a meet set up.'

'It's 10 o'clock at night Justin.'

'Tom, I need this bad, this is no joke. I'm serious as hell here.'

'K chill brutha, I got your back. Gimme half hour and I'll call you back on this number.'

'Cool, sweetness. My man.' They both hang up.

CHAPTER 16

REBELS

They arrive outside an underground bunker concealed from the main road. JC and Lucy meet up with JC's ex-agent; they embrace after seeing each other for the first time in months. They approach a steel door to a run-down building. Tom knocks on the door, and within a few seconds a slot opens up head high.

'What you want?' A big scary looking African-American peeps through the metal hole.

Tom steps forward 'it's Tom Wilkins here; I'm old pals of Jenny and Hector's. Uh, we have an invite.'

'Password?'

He looks sheepish as he says it, 'rubber baby ducky likes to fucky funnily.' Talk about tongue twisters. Tom turns to JC and Lucy then shrugs. Lucy giggles and squeezes JC's hand. He smirks in return. The large steel door opens slowly after a series of locks are heard.

'Come on in folks.'

The guard aka Big Joe stands aside as they enter. As they pass the huge man, they smile and Lucy gives a little wave.

'Follow the path, they're expecting you.'

'Thanks.'

They continue down the dark corridor lit only by work lights along every 10 metres. They eventually come to on open hall filled with computers, cables running everywhere, plastic sheets even some spare construction tools. Hector and Jenny Plaza are standing crouched over what looks like a command centre table in the middle of the room. As the three *outsiders* approach they see a whole team of people working around the room, as if a military operation. JC is reminded by this scene of his various army movies. Hector and Jenny look up as Tom shouts out.

'Hector, Jenny how the hell are ya?'

'It's been a while Tom.'

'Yeah man, where and how have you been?'

'Busy as hell till my buddy here was killed off in real life, not in the movies I might add.'

As Hector and Jenny approach them, they now recognize JC from film posters and some of his films. They have never officially met. Smiles appear on their focused faces. They reach out their hands to greet the film star and bypass Tom's open handshake.

'A pleasure to meet you Senor Case.'

'Likewise, I didn't know who else to call in an emergency than my agent. The irony, huh?'

They chuckle and look at Tom's face, in return he looks insulted. Hector notices Lucy standing nervously behind JC as if a shy child.

'And who do we have here then?'

JC tugs her from behind his back for her to come forward. She does not speak up yet. Hector's facial expression changes to slight recognition.

'Hang on, Senorita I recognize you for some reason. As if I haven't seen you in a long time or if-'

'She was a dead celebrity.'

Hector, Jenny and Tom look at her suspiciously. Then Hector recognizes her.

'No way! Is this a trip or what?'

Jenny catches on last, 'hang on, your shitting me right. Are you trying to tell me she's who I think she is?'

JC hums the theme for *I Love Lucy*. Lucy perks up as if recognizing the theme tune from her distant past.

'Lucille fucking Ball! I can't believe I didn't see it before, I guess it's a dark night. She is definitely the younger version for sure.' Tom catches on slow too.

'How is it possible? Dios mio (OMG).'

'It's a long story, you got a minute?'

'How about all night! I can't wait to hear this.'

JC sniffs the air, 'first, how about some fresh filter coffee? I haven't had any decent coffee in half a year.'

Lucy had never tried it on the island, 'real coffee?' They all look at her forgetting her innocence for a moment. For her sake, they only ever had instant coffee available. As a clone she didn't have the need to drink it, however.

'Yeah shit I forgot. You've never had real coffee before have you?'

'I don't think so.'

Hector shouts out, 'Chavez, caffe por favor (coffee please).'

Chavez, an assistant is at his work station but jumps up immediately and starts the coffee brewing machine. He is actually quite good at coffee's he makes cappuccinos with fern leaves from the frothed milk. He brings them over to the main table on a tray and passes them out one by one. Lucy loves her mug and cups it for warmth in this dark dank environment. JC sips from his mug and compliments Chavez's coffee making skills. On the island there was only instant coffee, it keeps longer you see.

'Damn. Chavez is it? Muy Bueno (very good).'

'Gracias senor (thank you mister).'

'De nada amigo (you're welcome friend)' in nearly perfect Spanish.

Lucy smiles at this, having and now having an even bigger crush on JC than before. She has never heard him speak another language before let alone Spanish in a flawless accent. He probably learned it on one of his big films she thinks to herself.

Hector is growing impatient, 'down to business please.'

JC takes a deep breath. 'Kay, here it is, it all started when I was contacted by.....'

JC lays out the whole conspiracy of the celebrity island, the CEU and especially the bit about the cloned politicians. Jenny tests Lucy's blood in the meantime; Lucy winces when the needle pokes the skin. They have the test results in minutes. They look at her blood count information on the big touchscreen computer monitor that is the table they sit around. A bunch of technical data regarding her DNA can be seen on the screen also.

Hector squints at the data, 'looks like here we have some rather strange results aqui (here).'

Justin takes a sarcastic tone like Bruce Campbell in his films, 'define strange? It's not like I haven't had enough of that lately.' Lucy chuckles quietly.

Hector continues, 'her DNA pattern does not match a conventional human. See this here (pointing at her broken DNA), this means she only has a life expectancy of 1 month.

'We know that already. The clones are all given shots once a month to recover the dying DNA.'

'Si, do you have any of this formula?'

JC turns to Lucy, 'yeah, which reminds me it's time for your shot babe.'

'Kay babe.'

'I got some spare; I'll hook you up in a sec.'

Lucy takes out a high tech syringe from her bag and passes it to JC, who gets her dose ready. He gives her the shot. He reaches into his backpack and passes a spare vile to Hector, who passes it to Jenny. They are quite the team. The analysis is done within seconds.

'Ah, si (yes). This explains it.'

The others all stare at the screens not able to understand what Hector sees.

'What?'

'This formula tricks the dying cells into thinking they are still alive, but cannot reproduce healthy cells only recreate or restructure the old ones.'

'You saying she's immortal, like a zombie?'

'Zombie? No. Immortal? (pause) Semi.'

'Semi? What the hell does that mean?'

'As in, she has an expiry date where the cells eventually get worn out and stop reproducing.'

'And how long would that be?' Justin showing some genuine concern for his *partner*.

'Who knows? Fifty years? A hundred? I mean I didn't even know about this tech until just now.'

'So Hector. Is what you've seen here tonight, can we build a case against these bastards or what?'

'More than a case Senor. We have a revolution on our hands.'

A big grin appears on JC's face, 'that's what I wanna hear.' JC stands up in a dramatic moment and holds out his hand like in the film *Predator*. Hector embraces the arm grabbing it and they smile.

Justin imitating Arnie from the film, 'what's ze matta? The CIA got you pushing too many penzils.'

'Predator baby. Claro (of course).'

All around the table, everyone else smiles at this cheesy yet monumental moment between the two grown men acting like kids. Hector gets serious again and stands up straight, JC does too.

Hector breaking from the moment, 'so do you have a plan yet?'

Defeated, they each sit back down slowly.

Justin looking around at everyone's faces, 'my plan was getting us here. Now we can talk shop and make a proper one on how to take this corrupt system down.'

'OK, what assets do you have?' Hector sees a bright and positive future.

'Just us and you.'

'Guns?'

'If we need them.'

'Explosives.'

'I know where to get some parts and can make C4 myself. I've had some practice recently.' JC smiles at Lucy sharing their private joke.

'So I suggest we start with a viral video, but first we need more information. You remember the building where you were offered this deal?'

'Of course I'll never forget it.'

'OK, we hit them first, see if we can get data and then we go global.'

Tom looks nervous not sure what he got himself into. 'Um guys, I made the introduction. You don't need me to stay any longer do you?'

JC turns to him placing his hand on Tom's shoulder, 'you're part of the team now Tom, we need every helping hand we can get.'

'Maybe I can be your man on the outside? If you need some materials or other stuff I can help.'

Hector nods in agreement, 'not a bad idea hefe (boss).'

'Maybe you're right. Let's go through the plan again, in proper detail this time and thoroughly.'

The five of them sit around leaning over the screen checking maps, locations terrain data, etc.

Later that night at the CEU HQ they raid then destroy the servers in the CEU building. They get all the info they need to take this branch of government down for good. They use sleeping darts on the guards and EMP guns (home-made) to take out the cameras. The hackers get to work immediately dealing with the security system, firewalls and any other issues along the way. Surprisingly no secret alarm is tripped and they are in an out within an hour. Justin reminisces when they walk along the same corridors as to the meeting that changed his life for good. The whole mission went off without a hitch, it was all too easy. Maybe just really good planning, but something didn't feel right to JC. He wasn't sad to see this place go, but in the back of his mind he knows there will be consequences though.

CHAPTER 17

VIRAL

Back in the underground bunker HD Cameras are set up to begin filming JC standing in front of a green screen background and a monitor/TV off to the side. The set-up matches a weather reporter in a TV studio. Lucy is applying some make up to JC's face. After she's done he grabs Lucy and swings her for an old fashioned film kiss as Hector and Jenny stand by the cameras waiting. They are about to film the viral video that will be posted online all over the world on various sites. They have a series of computer nerds hacking internet mainframes and re-routing their IP address so they cannot be shut down or intercepted for that period of time. JC strokes his hand through his hair licking his lips as Lucy looks at him adoringly like the star he still is.

Hector running out of patience as usual, 'ready Justin?'

JC casually, 'si senor.'

Hector counts down, '3 - 2 - 1.' Hector gives a thumbs up to signal he's rolling.

'I am Justin Case; most of you will know me from my action blockbuster films. I am not dead but still very alive as you can see. This is no trick or CG, computer graphics for laymans. Ladies and gentleman of the public, a great fraud has been committed in the US and most likely elsewhere in the world. I have substantial evidence of a secret cloning facility hidden in the Bermuda triangle. I was there. I was a dead celebrity like the rest, the only difference was that I wasn't really dead yet. A work in progress you might have called me. I was supposed to die on that island. I just had to expose this truth to the world. I bring you the biggest lie ever put upon the public of this once great country. Not only celebrities but politicians were made secretly on that island too. I'm not sure if I can navigate my way back there, but I know this: I will not leave my friends behind. They say they died young for a reason, but I say to you, they keep living regardless.'

Lucy smiles from the side off camera. JC waves her to come over. She obliges and stands next to him; he places his arm around her shoulder. On the green-screen behind images of her DNA strain are displayed and other technical data.

JC continues with his epic speech, 'this is Lucille Ball; you might remember her from the show *I Love Lucy* many decades ago. She is now my sweetheart. Can you imagine the possibilities? The island is still out there. (He points to the green screen) He sees a rough pre-viz (pre-visualisation) on a screen facing him next to the camera. No teleprompter here for his lines, it's all coming from the heart. The transition goes from JC to play the intro/demo video, first shown to him during the CEU meeting with the board. We cut to the video one last time. JC comes back into frame.

'You see, this place is real as am I standing here right now. (Hector's camera zooms in for a close up on JC) I used to be a movie star now all I wanna be is a hero to the people. Clones and humans alike. It's up to you now world, your move next.'

ENDING # 1 (HAPPY POTENTIAL SEQUEL ENDING)

- SPOLIER ALERT -

IF YOU LIKE HAPPY ENDINGS STOP READING NOW
HOWEVER IF YOU'RE CURIOUS TO SEE
WHAT THE ORIGINAL ENDING IS
KEEP GOING…

CHAPTER 18

DOOMED

The story continues as Hector stops rolling and calls cut. Lucy and JC hug and kiss again, like little love birds. Hector and Jenny make sure the video is safe and hands it to one of the computer tech guys. He does a quick edit adding in the background VFX. The filming was pre-viz only, but in five minutes or so they get to watch the finished product. Chavez starts switching off the stage lights for the TV set and powers down the cameras. Hector and Jenny wait eagerly by the editing station. JC and Lucy are still smooching on the TV set, Chavez looks jealous. Hector cheers as the video is being rendered taking only a minute. Fast computers are a must in his line of work.

'Heh amigo! We can upload in a few seconds. How about you do the honours?'

JC looks over to Hector and takes Lucy's hand leading her over to the editing station. The video editor sends the feed over to the big table so it all seems more dramatic. The upload option is flashing on the big table screen.

'Man I wish Tom was here to see this. I mean without him all this wouldn't have come together.'

Jenny looks around the room, 'where is Tom anyways? Why isn't he here?'

JC shrugs, 'dunno, he had some big meeting with some suits.'

Hector slaps JC on the arm, 'this is part of history amigo. We can't start a revolution without a cause. And boy do you have one.'

'Gracias Hector. I just wanna say thanks again for all your help.'

'De nada man.'

JC is grinning as he reaches for the upload touchscreen option. Just at that moment the power cuts out and the big steel door at the front of their base is blown open by a SWAT team. The explosion kills big Joe (the security guard) instantly. He didn't even expect it.

Emergency lighting kicks in, but all screens are blank. Some sparks come from the lights and computers. A wall security monitor still works due to the emergency power.

'What the hell was that? Chavez!'

'No say (I dunno) senor! I will try to get the back-up genie running.'

'Bueno, do it fast!'

Jenny can see movement on one of the working security monitors 'They're coming in!'

Hector is already heading towards a gun rack on the wall 'How many?'

'We gotta get outta here! You got a back door?' Justin calls out.

Hector looking heroic grabs a machine gun nearby; he tosses an M-16 (with grenade launcher attachment) to JC, while grabbing another one for himself. JC catches it. Jenny grabs an MP-5. 'Follow me, everyone out!'

Hector defies his wife's order. 'I'm staying!'

'No hefe no!' Jenny cries out.

'Lo siento (I'm Sorry) mi Jenita! I will hold them off for you!'

She pleads with him some more, 'come with us!'

'It's OK mi amore (my love).'

JC drags Jenny off of Hector. 'OK we gotta move, let's go!'

Right then gunshots rain out all over the hall cutting up the computers, the set, cameras everything. Some of the technicians get shot in the process. Hector ducks behind the big screen table and starts firing blindly at the invaders. JC helps out with firing a few rounds off, hitting a couple SWAT guys in the chest. The SWAT team hunker down to find some cover.

The side room is actually a storm drain JC, Lucy, Jenny and the remaining surviving technicians make it to the back room which has a tall metal grate at the top. The others start climbing up, while JC helps them grab onto the ladder. Lucy starts climbing following the crowd. Only JC and Jenny are left standing at the bottom of the ladder. There are flak vests, guns and extra ammo hanging on the wall nearby. JC sees grenades for his launcher attachment; he grabs them and loads one. Jenny grabs a flak vest; she puts it on as she talks.

'I'm going back in!'

'There's a whole SWAT team in there!'

'I don't wanna leave Hector to die! I'd rather go with him!'

'You're right, let's go. Me first, you follow and cover my back.' JC puts on a flak vest also and reloads his gun. Jenny charges out first ahead of JC.

Jenny and JC burst back into the room; JC chucks a grenade that he has strapped to his flak vest. They take out some more SWAT guys and a stand-off ensues and all parties are firing blindly not hitting any of their targets. Until JC gets a head shot, the SWAT unit seem to back off at first, but then armoured shielded riot police officers enter the arena. An M60 (Rambo's main gun) is heard firing towards them as cover for the riot police squad. JC, Hector and Jenny can't see the soldier, but the bullets rip through more tables, chairs, extra debris. Hector is hit in the leg in the process, Jenny runs over to him, trying to drag him out while bullets rain all over the place. JC tries his grenade launcher built into his M16 rifle.

Justin imitates Al Pacino in *Scarface* shouting out, 'say hello to my little friend!' He launches the grenade, which makes the usual THUMP sound first, then BOOM! It takes out part of the corridor leading to the main entrance. Smoke and debris is blocking the view. Shouts are heard, some screams. The building structure in the corridor is collapsing. The M60 has seized firing for now. In the clear, JC rushes over to Hector, who is bleeding badly. Jenny is crying holding her partner very concerned. JC leans in to help out;

he picks him up by one arm while Jenny supports his other shoulder. They slowly walk over to the back exit room. Then the power to the facility kicks back in.

'Viva! Chavez did it! He got the back-up generator working!'

'Go Chavez! That kid makes one hell of a coffee!'

There is smoke throughout the room making visibility poor and the trio have virtually forgotten about their pursuers in the meantime. They limp back to the main console. That's when a red laser beam can be seen flicking around in the haze. As if in slow motion, sniper rounds hit Hector and Jenny in the sides of their heads and they all collapse in a heap. Damn that sniper, he probably had thermal vision on his scope, Justin thinks to himself. JC is unharmed but it doesn't look good for Jenny and Hector, sniper rounds are bigger bullets and have taken them both out with massive exit wounds. They were dead instantly. At least she got her wish, they went out together.

JC hides behind some debris on the ground; he crawls over to the centre table which is working again. The screen is cracked but the upload option is still available. It flashes like an emergency light since most of the house lights have been shot out already. He reaches up off the floor and smacks the table a couple times, but no response. The touch screen has been disabled, the image is flickering. He stands up fires off a view rounds into the tunnel. While ducking and weaving, he pounds with his fist on the side panel, which is supposed to act like a giant mouse clicker. This works, the upload begins saying it will last up to a minute. Shouting is heard from the debris in the tunnel. Another hail of bullets fly through the room, JC shoots back but is hit by multiple bullets and shrapnel. It's as if the whole SWAT team was back for revenge. They don't let up: sniper rounds automatic machine gun fire even hand guns are fired, guess the M60 was out of bullets or incapacitated. JC stands for a while defiantly then is knocked back to the floor, covered in bullet wounds and bleeding all over, he coughs up blood. He is dying, but at least he has done it. The viral video is out there now, everyone served their purpose. Hector and Jenny died for this cause; looks like JC was gonna follow them soon. Images of the island, the various celebrities and Lucy flash through his mind. What will happen to them? Is the mission a success?

Since the machine gun was shot out of his hands, JC's reaches for a nearby hand gun. He manages to grab it weakly and hold it up towards his attackers. He chokes on his blood once more. His vision is blurring and fading in and out of black. He breathes his last breath and speaks his last words.

'Just-in-case.'

His hand falls to the ground still holding the gun.

ENDING # 2 (SAD NO SEQUEL ENDING)

27 Club:

1) Jean-Michel Basquait – Artist - Drug Overdose (Heroin)
2) Kurt Cobain – Nirvana – Suicide Shotgun to the head
3) Jimi Hendrix – The Experience – Choked on own vomit (Heroin)
4) Brian Jones – Rolling Stones – Drowned due to Drugs
5) Janis Joplin – Solo artist - Drug Overdose (Heroin)
6) Jim Morrison – The Doors – Drug Overdose (Heroin)
7) Amy Winehouse – Solo artist – Alcohol poisoning
8) Anton Yelchin – Actor - Accident
9) Many others (not as famous as list above)

Random International Deaths/causes & Ages:

1) Ian Curtis – Joy Division - Suicide by hanging - 23
2) Princess of Wales Lady Diana – Royalty - Car crash – 36
3) Ryan Dunn – *Jackass* - Car crash – 34
4) Bobby Kennedy – Politician - Assassination – 42
5) John F. Kennedy – President of USA - Assassination – 46
6) Martin Luther King Jr. – Activist - Assassination – 39
7) Brandon Lee – Action actor - Accidental Gunshot (*The Crow*) – 28
8) Bruce Lee – Action actor - Allergic reaction to a tranquilizer – 32
9) Bob Marley – Reggae Musician - Cancer – 36
10) Marilyn Monroe – Actress - Accidental overdose – 36
11) Brittany Murphy – Actress - Sickness - 32
12) Elvis Presley – Musician/Actor - Heart Attack – 42
13) 2Pac Shakur – Rapper/musician - Rival Assassination – 25
14) Paul Walker – Actor (*Fast & Furious*) - Car crash – 40
15) John Lennon - Beatles Musician - Assassination (gunshot)
16) Malcolm X - Activist - Assassination (gunshot)

Famous Actors I've filmed/worked/met with:

1) Danny Glover (x2) - Planet Hollywood (Jakarta) + LAX (Los Angeles Airport)
2) Sly Stallone - Planet Hollywood (Jakarta, Indonesia)
3) Jude Law x2 - outside LFS (Covent Garden) & *SH2: Game of Shadows* (London)
4) Hugo Weaving x2 - *V 4 Vendetta* (Hatfield) & *Hugo* whilst *Capt. America* (Shepperton)
5) Timothy Spall (*Turner/Secrets & Lies/HP*) – *The Last Hangman*
6) Eddie Marson x2 (*Vera Drake*) – *The Last Hangman* & *66**
7) James Franco (x2) - *Flyboys* & *Annapolis* (Greenwich)
8) Toby Stephens (Bond 20) – *Margaret* (London)
9) Bill Nighy (*Pirates 2&3*) - *Girl in a Café* (London)
10) Kelly McDonald (*Trainspotting/Boardwalk Empire/Choke*) - *Girl in a Café* (London)
11) Rick Mayall (*Drop Dead Fred*) - *All About George** (London)
12) Amy Smart (*Crank/Butterfly Effect*) - *Best Man* (Harrods, London)
13) Stuart Townsend (*Queen of the Damned*) - *Best Man* (Harrods, London)
14) Daniel Radcliffe - *HP 4: Goblet of Fire* (Leavesden studios)
15) Emma Watson - *HP 4: Goblet of Fire* (Leavesden studios)
16) Rupert Grint - *HP 4: Goblet of Fire* (Leavesden studios)
17) Domhnall Gleeson (Weasley brother) - *HP 4: Goblet of Fire* (Leavesden studios)
18) Bonnie Wright (Ginny Weasley) - *HP 4: Goblet of Fire* (Leavesden studios)
19) John Malkovich x2 - *Hitchhiker's Guide** & *Red 2* (London)
20) Martin Freeman x3 - *Hitchhiker's Guide* & *Sherlock* 1&3 (London)
21) Liam Neeson x2 - *Batman Begins* (Training in Shepperton) & *Clash 2* (Wales)

22) Christian Bale - *Batman Begins* (Training in Shepperton studios)
23) Katie Holmes - *Batman Begins* (Shepperton studios)
24) Stephen Marcus (*Lock Stock*) - *Kinky Boots* (Soho)
25) Chiwetel Ejifor x2 (*Serenity/2012*) - *Kinky Boots* (Soho) & Pangea Project* (London)
26) Nick Frost (*Shaun of the Dead/Spaced*) x2 - *Kinky Boots* & *Money* (Pinewood studios)
27) Michelle Pfeiffer x2 - *I Could Never* (London) & *Dark Shadows* (Pinewood)
28) Paul Rudd - *I Could Never* (Battersea club)
29) Tyrese Gibson (*Fast & Furious*) – *Annapolis* (Greenwich)
30) Jordanna Brewster (*Fast & Furious*) – *Annapolis* (Greenwich)
31) Kirsten Dunst (*Spiderman* 1-3)– *Wimbledon* (real location)
32) Jared Harris (*SH2*) - Leicester Square (London)
33) Judi Dench - *Notes on a Scandal* (London)
34) Cate Blanchett - *Notes on a Scandal* (London)
35) Jean Reno (*Leon*) - *Da Vinci Code* (Shepperton)
36) Alessandro Nivola (*Face Off*) – *Goal* (Fulham Stadium)
37) Kuno Becker – *Goal* (Fulham Stadium)
38) Kate Winslett – *Holiday* (Embankment)
39) Tracey Ulman x2 - *I Could Never* (London) & *Tracey Ullman Show* TV
40) Reese Witherspoon - *Penelope** (London)
41) Christina Richi x2 - *Penelope** & *Bel Ami** (London)
42) Richard E. Grant – *Penelope* (London)
43) Catherine O'Hara – *Penelope* (London)
44) Joss Ackland – *Flawless* (London)
45) Robert De Niro - *Stardust* (Pinewood & loc)
46) Claire Danes - *Stardust* (Pinewood & loc)
47) Sienna Miller - *Stardust* (Pinewood & loc)
48) Dexter Fletcher x2 - *Stardust* (Pinewood & loc) & *Eddie the Eagle* (as Director)*
49) Carmen Electra – *I Want Candy (Ealing)**

50) Tom Burke (*Donkey Punch*) x2 – *I Want Candy (Ealing) & Invisible Woman* premiere
51) Tom Riley (*Davinci's Demons*) - *I Want Candy (Ealing)*
52) Jamie Bamber (*Battelstar Galatica*) – *Law & Order 2* (Longcross)
53) John Cusack - *1408* (Elstree studios & Pall Mall loc)
54) Samuel L. Jackson - *1408* (Pall Mall)
55) Robert Carlisle (*Trainspotting*) - *28 Weeks Later*
56) Cliff Curtis x2 (*Once Were Warriors & Die Hard 4.0*) – Maori Screening* & NZ Film Commission*
57) Julian Arahanga (*Once Were Warriors*) – Whenua/Maori Films screening
58) Thomas Robins (Deagol in *LOTR*) - Kaitoke Park (Rivendell)*
59) John Rhys-Davies (Gimli in *LOTR*) - Armageddon Comic Expo* (Welly)
60) Billy Dee Williams (*Lando* in *Star Wars*) – Armageddon Expo* (Welly)
61) Don S. Davis (Gen Hammond *Stargate* TV) - Armageddon Expo (Welly)
62) Aaron Douglas (*Battlestar Galactica*) - Armageddon Expo (Welly)
63) Stephen Lang (*Gods & Generals/Gettysburg*) - *Avatar** (Stone St, Wellywood)
64) Giovanni Ribisi – *Avatar* (Stone St, Wellywood)
65) Sam Worthington (*Terminator: Salvation*) x2 - *Avatar** (Stone St, Welly) & *Clash 2* (Wales)
66) Sigourney Weaver - *Avatar** (Stone St, Welly)
67) Matt Gerald (*Daredevil* TV) – *Avatar* (Stone St, Wellywood)
68) D'Leep Rao (*Drag me to Hell*) - *Avatar** (Stone St, Wellywood)
69) Michelle Rodrigez (*Fast & Furious*) – *Avatar* (Stone St, Wellywood)
70) Joel David Moore (*Dodge Ball*) - *Avatar** (Stone St, Wellywood)

71) Sean Anthony Moran (Pvt. Fike in *Avatar*) – *Avatar**
72) Scott Lawrence (Various TV) – *Avatar*
73) Ryan Gosling - Auckland airport (NZ)
74) T (Boogie in *Once were Warriors*) - *Avatar** (Wellywood)
75) Nathan Meister (*Black Sheep*) - *Avatar** (Stone St, Wellywood)
76) Coen Holloway x2 (*Eagle vs. Shark*) - *Avatar*/TV Drama*
77) Russell Crowe - *Robin Hood* (Shepperton back-lot)
78) Kevin Durand - *Robin Hood* (Shepperton back-lot)
79) Oscar Isaac x2 - *Robin Hood* (Shepperton back-lot) & *W.E.* (London)
80) Lea Seydoux (*Spectre/Blue is the Warmest Color*) - *Robin Hood*
81) Mark Strong *(Kingsman/Welcome to Punch)* - *Robin Hood*
82) Ben Kingsley - *Hugo* (Shepperton)
83) Christopher Lee - *Hugo* (Shepperton)
84) Chloe Grace Moretz (*Kick Ass*) - *Hugo* (Shepperton)
85) Asa Butterfield (*Enders Game*) – *Hugo* (Shepperton)
86) Richard Griffiths (*HP all*) - *Hugo* (Shepperton)
87) Francis de la Tur (*HP 4*) - *Hugo* (Shepperton)
88) Sacha Baron Cohen x2 (*Ali G/Borat/Bruno*) – *Hugo* (Shepperton) & *Bros Grimsby* (Greenwich)
89) Emily Mortimer (*Lars and the Real Girl*) - *Hugo* (Shepperton)
90) Rose Byrne (*Bad Neighbours 1&2/Get Him to the Greek*) - *X-Men: 1st Class* (Café de Paris)
91) January Jones (*Mad Men*) - *X-Men: 1st Class* (Café de Paris)
92) Jeremy Irvine x2 - *War Horse* (Wisley) & *Great Expectations* (Gillette Factory)
93) Johnny Depp - *Dark Shadows* (Pinewood)
94) Eva Green - *Dark Shadows* (Pinewood)
95) Johnny Lee Miller – *Dark Shadows* (Pinewood)
96) Toby Kebell x3 (*Rock n Rolla*) - *War Horse* (Wisley) & *Clash 2* (Wales) & *Escape Artist* (London)
97) Rosamund Pike – *Wrath of the Titans* aka *Clash 2* (Wales)
98) Ralph Fiennes x3 - *Wrath of the Titans* aka *Clash 2* (Wales) & *Invisible Woman** & London premiere

100) Kristen Stewart (*Twilight*) - *Snow White & the Hunstman* (Pinewood)
101) Ian McShane (*Deadwood* TV) - *Snow White & the Hunstman* (Pinewood)
102) Chris Hemsworth (*Thor/Avengers*) - *Snow White & the Hunstman* (Pinewood)
103) Charlize Theron - *Snow White & the Hunstman* (Pinewood)
104) Edward Furlong (*Terminator 2*) - *Zombie King* (Gaffer/Crew-Somerset)*
105) Corey Feldman (*Lost Boys*) - *Zombie King* (Gaffer/Crew-Somerset)*
106) Riz Ahmed (*Nightcrawler*) x2 – XOYO Adam F gig (MC Riz)* & *Jason Bourne* (5)
107) Anna Friel – *Look of Love*
108) Steve Coogan (*Alan Partridge*) - *Look of Love*
109) Imogen Poots (*28 Weeks Later*) - *Look of Love*
110) Tamsin Egerton (*St Trinian's* & *4321*) - *Look of Love*
111) David Walliams (Comedian) - *Look of Love*
112) Kristin Scott Thomas x2 – *Invisible Woman* & London premiere (Odeon Kens.)
113) Sharlto Copley (*A-Team/District 9/Elysium/Chappie*) – *Maleficent* (Pinewood)
114) Tom Wilkinson (*Batman Begins*) – *Belle* (Oxford)
115) Bruce Willis – *Red 2* (Hemel Hempstead)
116) Paul Kaye (*All Gone Pete Tong*) – Bet Victor Ad (Charlton FC)*
117) Kiran Shah (Scale double 4 Frodo/Bilbo) - Bet Victor Ad (Charlton FC)*
118) Bradley Walsh x3 (*Lock Stock TV*) – *Law & Order* UK*
119) Idris Elba (*Prometheus/The Wire/Thor*) – *Luther Season 3*ature* (London loc)
120) Warren Brown (*Dark Knight*) - *Luther Season 3* (London loc)
121) David Tennant (*Dr. Who*) – *Escape Artist*
122) Ricky Gervais x2 (*Extras/Office*) – *Life's Too Short & Life on the Road* (DB driving double)*

123) Stephen Merchant (*Extras/Office*) - *Life's Too Short*
124) Warwick Davis (*Willow/HP*) - *Life's Too Short*
125) Derren Brown (Illusionist) – *Sherlock* SE3 EP1
126) Benedict Cumberbatch x2 – *Sherlock* SE1EP1 & SE3 EP1
127) Andrew Scott (Moriaty) – *Sherlock* SE3 EP1*
130) Mark Gatiss (Mycroft) – *Sherlock* SE3 EP1*
131) Louise Brealey - *Sherlock* SE3 EP1*
132) Nicolas Lyndhurst (*Only Fools & Horses*) – *New Tricks*
133) Denis Waterman (OG *The Sweeney*) – *New Tricks*
134) Tamsin Outhwaite (*Eastenders*) – *New Tricks*
135) Denis Lawson (*Star Wars*) – *New Tricks*
136) Alun Armstrong - *New Tricks*
137) Christopher Eccleston (*Thor 2 & Gone in 60 Secs*) – *Lucan*
138) Henry Cavill (*Batman vs Superman/Man of Steel*) – *Man from UNCLE*
139) Armie Hammer (*Lone Ranger/Social Network*) - *Man from UNCLE*
140) Alan Davies (*QI*) – *Jonathan Creek* (TV)
141) Sarah Alexander - *Jonathan Creek* (TV)
142) Imelda Staunton (*Vera Drake* & *HP*) – *Pride*
143) Felicity Jones x2 (*Breathe In*) – *Invisible Woman* & London premiere*
144) Tom Hollander (*Pirates of Caribbean*) – *Invisible Woman*
145) Simon Pegg x3 – *Man Up* (Waterloo) *Absolutely Anything* (London) & *MI5* (Leavesden)
146) Lake Bell (*In a World/Black Rock*) – *Man Up* (Waterloo)
147) Gary Oldman – *Robocop* premiere (IMAX)
148) Joel Kinneman (*The Killing/Run All Night*) – Robocop premiere (IMAX)
149) Abbie Cornish (*Bright Star*) x2 – *W.E.* (London) & Robocop premiere (IMAX)
150) Bill Bailey (Comedian) – Robocop premiere* (IMAX)
151) Kiefer Sutherland – *24* (Walton)
152) Yvonne Stahovski (*Dexter* TV) - *24* (Walton)
153) Alex Kingston (*ER/Boudica*) – *Chasing Shadows* (Woolwich)

154) Noel Clarke (*Kid/Bro/Adulthood*) - *Chasing Shadows* (Woolwich)*
155) Lorraine Stanley x2 (*London to Brighton*) – *Devils Dosh* (Crew) & *Chasing Shadows* (Woolwich)*
156) Sean Harris (*Prometheus*) – *Macbeth* (Surrey)
157) Michael Fassbender x2 – *SH: Case of Silk Stocking & Macbeth* (Surrey)
158) Ralph Brown (*Alien 3*) – *Babylon* (London location)*
159) Rose Leslie (Igrit *Game of Thrones*) – *The Great Fire* (Oxfordshire)
160) Kit Harrington (Jon Snow *GOT*) – *Spooks: Greater Good* Film (London)
161) Brit Marling (*Another Earth*) – *Babylon* (London location)
162) Patterson Joseph (*Peep Show*) x2 – *Babylon* (London location) & You, Me & the *Apocalypse**
163) John Hannah (*Mummy* 1-3) – *Valentine's Kiss* (Denham location)
164) Rupert Graves (Lestrade in *Sherlock*) – *Valentine's Kiss* (Denham location)
165) Clive Swift (*Keeping Up Appearances*) – *Valentine's Kiss* (Denham location)
166) Ben Chaplin (*Thin Red Line*) – *Tarzan* (Leavesden studios) training
167) Scott Adkins (*Ninja* 1&2) – *Brothers Grimsby*
168) Tom Hardy (Bane in *Batman 3/Warrior*) – *Legend*
169) Emily Browning (*Sucker Punch/Pompeii*) – *Legend*
170) Paul Anderson (*Peaky Blinders/Piggy*) – *Legend*
171) Adam Fogerty x2 (*Snatch/Stardust*) – *Legend & Stardust*
172) Christoph Waltz (*Inglorious Basterds*) – *Legend of Tarzan (Leavesden studios)*
173) Margot Robbie (*Wolf of Wall St*) - *Legend of Tarzan (Leavesden studios)*
174) Casper Crump (Vandall Savage from *Arrow/Legends of Tomorrow*) – *Legend of Tarzan*
175) Mia Wasikowska (*Alice*) – *Alice in Wonderland 2* (Shepperton)

176) Ed Speelers (*Eragon*) – *Alice in Wonderland 2*
177) Lindsay Duncan (*Alice*) – *Alice in Wonderland 2* (Shepperton)
178) Tom Cruise – *MI5: Rogue Nation (Leavesden)*
179) Jeremy Renner (*Avengers/Hurt Locker*)– *MI5: Rogue Nation (Leavesden)*
180) Ving Rames (*Pulp Fiction*) – *MI5: Rogue Nation (Leavesden)*
181) Alec Baldwin – *MI5: Rogue Nation (Leavesden)*
182) David Morissey (*Walking Dead* TV/*Basic Instinct 2*) x2 – *Blackpool* (TV) & Stokey
183) Ade (*Snatch*) – Sports Direct (Stokey)
184) Stellan Skaarsgard – *River* TV (London location)
185) John Simms (*Human Traffic & Life on Mars*) – *Code of a Killer* (London location)
186) Chuck Venn (Eastenders) – MTA (*Meet the Adebanjos*) SE2
187) Kayvan Novak (*Fone/Facejacker*) – *Suntrap* (3 Mills Studio)
188) Sophie Okenedo (*Hotel Rwanda/Aeon Flux*) – *Hollow Crown* (Kent)*
189) Tom Sturridge (*The Boat that Rocked/On the Road*)- *Hollow Crown* (Kent)
190) Morgan Freeman (*Seven/Shawshank Redemption*) - *Now You See Me 2* (Surrey)
191) Aml Ameen (*Maze Runner*) – Commonwealth Youth Q&A (Marlboro house)
192) Taron Egerton (*Kingsman*) – *Eddie The Eagle* (Pinewood)
193) Russell Howard (Comedian) – *Gert A Lush X-Mas* (TV Show)
194) Neil Morrissey (*Men Behaving Badly*) – *Gert A Lush X-Mas* (TV Show)*
195) Jim Howick (Comedian) – Stag (Loc)
196) Stephen Campbell Moore – Stag (Loc)
197) Ben Mendelshon (Aussie) – *Una* film (loc)
198) Tobias Menzies (Rome) - *Una* film (loc)
199) Indira Varma (*Rome/Game of Thrones*) - *Una* film (loc)
200) David Mitchel x2 (Comedian) – *All About George* & *Peep Show* (SE9)
201) Marc Webb (Comedian) – *Peep Show* (SE9)

202) Matt King (Supa Hands) – *Peep Show* (SE9)
203) Lesley Joseph (Dark Haired) – *Birds of a Feather* (SE12)*
204) Eddie Redmayne – *Fantastical Beasts & Where to Find Them* (Leavesden studios)
205) Ezra Miller - *Fantastical Beasts & Where to Find Them* (Leavesden studios)
206) Samantha Morton - *Fantastical Beasts & Where to Find Them* (Leavesden studios)
207) Brad Pitt x2 - *War Machine* (2015) & *Allied* (2016)
208) Marianne Coultard - *Allied* (2016)
209) Jared Harris x2 (SH2) - London streets & *Allied* (2016)*
210) Alan Rickman (*Die Hard/HP*) – A Little Chaos (*as Director*)
211) Charlotte Hope (*Game of Thrones*) x2 – *Irongate* (short)* & *Allied* (2016)*
211) Lizzy Kaplan (*Now You See Me 2*) – Allied (2016)
212) Don Johnson *(Miami Vice* TV 80s) – *Sick Note* (London)
213) Adrian Lester (*Day After 2Moro & Primary Colors*) – *Undercover* (London)
214) Kyle Soller (*Hollow Crown* SE2) – *You, Me & the Apocalypse* (2015)
215) Ella Smith (Big girl) x2 - *Babylon* & *Hoff the Record* SE2*
216) Lily James (*Pride, Prejudice & Zombies*) – *Downtown Abbey* SE5
217) George McKay (*11.22.63 & Pride*) – *Devil's Dosh* (Short film 60K)*
218) Steven Mulhern (Presenter/Comedian/magician) – *Go For It* (ITV game show)
219) Jamie Bell *(Billy Ellio/King Kong/Turn* TV) – *Film Stars don't Die in Liverpool*
220) Annette Benning (*American Beauty*) - *Film Stars don't Die in Liverpool*
221) Claire Foy (*Crossbones* TV) – *Breathe* (Luton loc)

* = I've spoken to
x3 = RIP

RIP TO ALL THOSE FALLEN COMRADES
IN THE FILM BUSINESS

THIS STORY IS IN HONOUR OF YOU ALL